W9-AXK-319

Shelby searched for something to say. "Matt, I—"

"You met my kids." His tone was flat and cool.

Shelby nodded, mentally scurrying to regain her footing at his abrupt change of subject. "They're adorable. I like their dog, too." She couldn't help but smile at the thought of them. "They were very well behaved. You and your wife should be proud. You've done a wonderful job with them."

Matt paled. His eyes turned dark and cold. "My wife died three years ago."

She gasped. "Oh, Matt. I didn't know. I'm so sorry." He pinned her with a cold blue glare.

"My kids have been through a lot. They're emotionally vulnerable and they tend to give their hearts too easily. I don't want those hearts broken by a stranger passing through town."

Stranger? Was that how he thought of her now? Before she could respond, he turned and walked to the door.

He stopped, looking over his shoulder. "Do we understand each other?"

LORRAINE BEATTY

was born and raised in Columbus, Ohio, but has been blessed to live in Germany, Connecticut and Baton Rouge. She now calls Mississippi home. She and her husband, Joe, have two sons and six grandchildren. Lorraine started writing in junior high and has written for trade books, newspapers and company newsletters. She is a member of RWA and ACFW and is a charter member and past president of Magnolia State Romance Writers. In her spare time she likes to work in her garden, travel and spend time with her family.

Rekindled Romance
Lorraine Beatty

HARLEQUIN® LOVE INSPIRED®

If you purchased this book without a cover you should be aware
that this book is stolen property. It was reported as "unsold and
destroyed" to the publisher, and neither the author nor the
publisher has received any payment for this "stripped book."

Recycling programs
for this product may
not exist in your area.

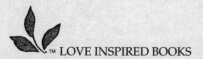

™ LOVE INSPIRED BOOKS

ISBN-13: 978-0-373-87810-9

REKINDLED ROMANCE

Copyright © 2013 by Lorraine Beatty

All rights reserved. Except for use in any review, the reproduction
or utilization of this work in whole or in part in any form by any
electronic, mechanical or other means, now known or hereafter
invented, including xerography, photocopying and recording, or in
any information storage or retrieval system, is forbidden without
the written permission of the editorial office, Love Inspired Books,
233 Broadway, New York, NY 10279 U.S.A.

This is a work of fiction. Names, characters, places and incidents are
either the product of the author's imagination or are used fictitiously, and
any resemblance to actual persons, living or dead, business establishments,
events or locales is entirely coincidental.

This edition published by arrangement with Love Inspired Books.

® and TM are trademarks of Love Inspired Books, used under license.
Trademarks indicated with ® are registered in the United States Patent
and Trademark Office, the Canadian Trade Marks Office and in other
countries.

www.LoveInspiredBooks.com

Printed in U.S.A.

A time to tear down and a time to build.
—*Ecclesiastes* 3:3

To my grandchildren: Cameron, Casie, Chey, Andrew, Anna and Addie. You are my treasures.

Chapter One

Shelby Russell steered her gray Malibu onto Highway 34 past the city limits sign of Dover, Mississippi, bracing herself against a sudden rush of painful memories. Coming home was the last thing she wanted to do. She'd turned her back on the small Southern town fifteen years ago and never looked back. Every goal she'd set for herself had been achieved. She'd risen through the ranks of Harmon Publishing to become senior editor of *Tween Scene* magazine, the top-selling publication for preteen girls in the country. It was a high-energy, high-stress job, and she loved every minute of it. But it was also the reason she was coming home.

Shelby eased the car to a halt behind a short line of cars waiting for a train to pass; the blinking red warning lights at the crossing were an unwelcome reminder of why she was back in Dover. A heart attack. She'd laughed in the doctor's face when he'd delivered his diagnosis. Heart attacks were for old people. She was only thirty-four. True, she'd had only a very mild one, but the tests didn't lie, and if she didn't eliminate the stress and change her lifestyle, she wouldn't be around to continue her exciting career. She'd already lost two grandfathers and an aunt to heart disease. She couldn't ignore her medical history.

The crossing gate lifted, and Shelby eased forward with the traffic. So here she was, coming home to stay with her grandmother, her life in chaos, her future in doubt. She was thankful that she had someone here who still cared about her, someone she could turn to when the world didn't make sense anymore. And right now, nothing did.

Her gaze surveyed the changes in the once-familiar surroundings as she followed the two-lane road toward town. The fields and piney woods surrounding the small town had been replaced with new shopping centers and an industrial park. A sprawling attendance center filled what once had been cotton fields. Courtesy of the new auto plant no doubt. Gramma had told her the plant, situated between the towns of Dover and Sawyers Bend, had brought about huge changes to both the once-dying towns.

As the highway gave way to downtown, the changes became more evident. The majestic courthouse still dominated the center of the town, but the surrounding trees were bigger and the elegant wrought-iron fence was a crisp shiny black. The historic gazebo, Dover's iconic symbol, still stood proudly in one corner of the grounds, like a Victorian jewel in the late-afternoon sunshine. The four streets flanking the square, lined with 19th-century brick buildings, all sported freshly painted facades in a variety of colors. Many storefronts had bright awnings providing shade; others had flower-draped balconies. The entire area looked like a water-color painting of the quintessential small Southern town. The Dover she remembered looked nothing like this.

Shelby pulled to a stop at the red light, willing herself not to look at the store on the corner, but the temptation was too great. Her gaze traveled to Durrant's Hardware. The real reason she'd stayed away so long. Matt Durrant was here. Her heart pounded. Was Matt in the store right now? Had he taken over the family business? Probably. It was the reason she'd left. They had wanted different things out of life. Incompatible things.

The light changed and she focused on the road ahead, trying to push all thoughts of Matt to the back of her mind. She failed. Did he ever think about her? Was he as handsome now as he'd been then? Had he married?

Gritting her teeth, Shelby forced all thoughts of Matt and the past aside and focused on making the turns that would take her to Willow Street. She pulled into Gramma's driveway and stopped, taking a moment to appreciate the two-story redbrick house. Nestled on a tree-lined street on the south edge of town, the foursquare-style home was a mirror image of the house next door. Their expansive lots butted up against the woodlands. Both homes had been built by Gramma's great-great-grandfather and his brother, who helped found the railroad town, then known as Junction City. Her heart warmed as she gazed upon the stately dwelling. The large front porch, the potted chrysanthemums and the massive live oak tree in the yard all welcomed her home.

Home.

Memories of feeling safe, loved and happy flowed through her even as tears burned behind her eyes. She'd left here so full of dreams, determined to conquer the world, but she was returning with her life in turmoil. Mentally she kicked herself for holding a pity party. She might be down, but she wasn't out. She would beat this. She would not let this health issue ruin her future. It was merely a matter of blocking out the fear and taking control of her life. She'd learn to relax. She'd learn to de-stress. She'd learn to be peaceful if it was the last thing she ever did.

Shelby let off the brake, guiding the car to the left of the Y-shaped driveway between the twin houses, and parked beneath the shade of a giant live oak. Her cramped muscles protested angrily as she unfolded herself from the vehicle, and a wave of exhaustion and defeat settled upon her shoulders. The long drive from New York to central Mississippi had been intended to give her time to relax and slow down. Instead, it had allowed too much time for regret and introspection. Neither of which eased her stress.

Gramma Bower burst through the front door and met her as Shelby topped the porch steps. Shelby's mood brightened at the sight of her grandmother's sweet face.

"Oh, my precious baby girl. I didn't think you'd ever get here."

Shelby went willingly into the warm, familiar hug, clinging to the woman who had been her refuge throughout her childhood. The loving embrace siphoned off much of her fatigue and eased her fears. Coming home to Gramma had been the right thing to do. She stepped back, taking a quick inventory. Gramma's hair was grayer, and there were more lines in her dear face. A few more pounds hugged the sturdy frame since she'd last seen her, but Gramma was still the same woman who had always loved her unconditionally.

"Child, let me look at you." She frowned. "You look tired."

Leave it to Gramma to get right to the heart of a matter. "I am. It was a long trip."

"Well, I know you said you needed to rest, but I had

no idea. You're pale as a ghost." Gramma shook her head. "Come on inside. I have sugar cookies for you."

The moment Shelby stepped inside the old house, her senses exploded with memories. She inhaled the familiar aroma of furniture polish, potpourri and fresh sugar cookies. The wood floors creaked a welcome beneath her feet as her fingers gently touched the worn spot on the newel post.

Her gaze quickly traveled around the rooms. Nothing had changed. The furnishings were still in the same place, as if time had stood still. Shelby soaked in the comfort of the old surroundings. Her own life might be in turmoil, but Gramma's house would always be her safe haven. "It's good to be home, Gramma. I've missed this place."

"Well, it's right where it's always been."

A lump of shame rose in her throat. "I know." Since leaving town, Shelby had stayed in touch with her grandmother and made the obligatory Christmas visits to her mother and stepfather's home in Pensacola, but she had staunchly avoided a visit to Dover. She couldn't risk running into Matt.

As they walked through the hallway, past the gallery of family photos, Shelby saw the picture of her aunt Teresa on the wall, and her conscience stung. She'd missed her aunt's funeral, her mother's only sister and a woman only ten years older than herself. *Tween Scene* magazine had been putting together their double Christmas issue at the time and that had seemed more important. Now Shelby winced at her callousness. "I'm sorry I didn't make it back for Aunt Teresa's funeral." Shelby followed her grandmother into the kitchen.

"I understood, baby. Really I did." Gramma smiled, handing her a plate of still-warm sugar cookies.

Shelby briefly thought about the dietary rules the doctor had laid out. Her mouth watered at the savory aroma, banishing her guilt. There was no need to start that healthy lifestyle right now. Tomorrow was soon enough. Sinking her teeth into one warm and sweet cookie transported her back in time. She was ten. Her father had deserted her and her mother. Shelby had run to Gramma's, scared, confused and in tears. Ellen had baked a batch of cookies and they'd talked and watched movies well into the night.

Gramma pointed at the plate and raised her eyebrows. "Eat up. Those might be the last ones you get for a while."

Shelby stopped midbite. "Why?"

"I work part-time at the church during the week, and I volunteer at the hospital whenever I'm needed. Besides—" Gramma planted her hands on her ample hips "—you're not supposed to be eating all that sugar."

Shelby pursed her lips. "I don't think a few cookies will do any harm."

Ellen frowned. "I see you haven't lost your habit of avoiding the unpleasant. Is this how you rose to the top of your field? By avoiding things?"

"No, of course not."

"You *are* following the doctors' instructions, aren't you? You're watching what you eat and exercising, taking your medications?"

Shelby reached for another cookie. The sample medications the doctor had given her had nearly run out, and the prescriptions were still in her purse. Filling them would make this whole thing too real. Too final. "I'm going to."

"Going to? When?" Gramma huffed out a puff of irritation. "Shelby Kay, you've got to take your heart disease seriously. This isn't something you can avoid. Baby. I've already lost a husband and a daughter. I don't want to lose you, too."

The pleading in her grandmother's voice punctured her defenses and exposed the gnawing fear in her spirit. Tears welled up in her eyes and clogged her throat. She was a lost and confused child again whose world was crashing in around her. Gramma's love was the only thing that had saved her. And God's grace.

She pressed her fingers to her lips as the fear took hold. "Gramma, I'm scared. How could I have had a heart attack and not even know it? I thought it was indigestion."

Gramma came to her side and pulled her shoulders. "Oh, my baby girl. I know. I'm sure the doctor explained to you that the symptoms are very different in women. But you can get through this if you'll just rely on the Lord."

Shelby shook her head. "It's not only my health, Gramma. The company I work for, Harmon Publishing, was bought by a competitor. I might not even have a job to go back to. The new management assured us everything would continue as before, but it's only a matter of time before the pink slips are handed out."

"I'm so sorry to hear that, but it's only a job, after all." Gramma squeezed her shoulders again. "It'll all work itself out."

Shelby pulled away, wiping her face with her palms and shaking her head. "It's more than a job. This magazine is my life."

Gramma scowled. "Nonsense."

"My career is who I am." Shelby stood and paced a few steps. "This is what I've worked for my whole life, and now I could lose everything." Shelby buried her head in her hands. Gramma came quickly to her side, patting her back.

"You don't know that. You're facing a lot of obstacles right now, but you have your brains and your experience. You can always find a job. This might be the best thing that ever happened to you."

Shelby gritted her teeth against the idea. "How could losing my career be a good thing?" Her grandmother stiffened, and Shelby realized how belligerent and disrespectful she'd sounded. "I'm sorry, Gramma. But I don't want to lose my job. It's important to me."

"Better your job than your life." Gramma stared down at her. "Seems to me, you've forgotten who to turn to when you're lost."

Shelby sank back down onto the wooden chair and tried to swallow her irritation. She wasn't surprised by her Gramma's comments. Her grandfather had been a minister. "Church talk" had been commonplace here. There had been a time when she had embraced her faith, depended upon it, but after she'd left Dover she'd drifted away. She'd channeled all her energy into school and then her career. Along the way she'd lost her connection to her faith.

Gramma patted her hand and slid the cookie plate toward her. "Enjoy your cookies. Today is your homecoming celebration. Tomorrow we'll face the changes you have to make."

Shelby nodded, feeling the fear and anger ease a bit. She had resisted coming back to Dover, but now she knew it had been the right decision. A few days here under Gramma's loving care would ease anyone's stress. A new hope blossomed in her heart. She had six weeks in which to accomplish her goals. First, get a handle on her health. Second, avoid Matt Durrant at all costs. That shouldn't be too difficult. She'd have no reason to go to his hardware store, and he lived on the opposite side of town. And maybe, if she could relax quickly enough, she could cut her leave in half and get back to work sooner, and that would decrease her odds of running into Matt.

Matthias Durrant. The only man she'd ever loved. They'd promised to love each other forever, to be together always, but it hadn't worked out that way. Matt had changed the plan, and she'd been terrified of losing her dream.

She'd never regretted her decision. So why did she find herself wondering what her life would have been like if she'd stayed here with him? Followed his dream instead of her own? There was no point in thinking about it. The door to the past was closed forever and couldn't be reopened.

Matt Durrant rested his wrists on the steering wheel of the old battered van, smiling as his passenger opened the door and got out. "Thanks for your help today, Carl."

The man nodded and raised a hand. "My pleasure. That roof should have been repaired months ago. We need more volunteers."

"Amen to that."

"Thanks for dropping me off at the house." Carl smiled. "It saved Nancy a trip to pick me up."

"No problem." Matt watched as his friend walked up the drive toward his house. The front door opened and his wife, Nancy, walked out to meet him, wrapping him in that special kind of hug only a wife could give. Matt looked away, ignoring the sudden ache in the center of his chest, and put the car in gear.

But the image replayed in his mind as he drove the

Handy Works van toward his home on the opposite side of town. He'd once had that kind of love. Until three years ago, when cancer had taken his Katie away. He called up a memory, looking for the comfort that normally soothed his wounded soul, but it didn't come. Instead he found a gray void.

For the first time he longed for a real moment, not a vision of what had been. His memories had sustained him, kept him afloat, but lately it had been harder and harder to find solace in the past. Seeing Carl and Nancy just now had cracked the protective wall around his heart, exposing his vulnerability. Loneliness.

He'd been lonely every second since Katie had died, but this was different. This was more like a yearning, a hunger for something more. He wasn't sure what it was exactly. His heart would always be missing the piece that Katie had filled. That first year he'd struggled to manage his grief against that of his children, trying to find a balance between keeping Katie's memory alive and not being crushed under the memory of her illness and death. The decision to leave Atlanta and move home to Dover had been another upheaval in their lives that couldn't be avoided. The pressures of his job had stolen precious time from his children. And they were his primary concern now.

Katie had begged him to not stop living after she was gone. She'd wanted him to find love and happiness again, but the thought had been abhorrent to him. He had no desire to risk his heart or his children's on that kind of loss again. None of them could survive it a second time. It's why he'd made the decision to come home. He wanted to raise his children near their grandparents, in a town where family values were still cherished.

Matt turned the corner onto Willow Street. Envy.

That's what had stirred up those old emotions. He was envious of Carl and Nancy's normal life. But he knew he had so much to be thankful for. Two amazing kids, a family that loved and supported him, a job that allowed him to be home a good bit—the van hit a pothole and every bolt rattled and shook. He smiled. And a ministry that helped the community and allowed him to help others. Handy Works had been his sister's brainchild. A mobile neighborhood help program, manned by volunteers who would donate their time and talents to making repairs and cleanup for those in need. He and his friend Carl Young had taken advantage of a rare afternoon free from teaching classes at Wells Community College to devote time to repairing the roof of an elderly man who lived at the edge of town.

Inhaling a deep breath, he reminded himself of his abundant blessings. Too many to count. This sudden feeling of loneliness would pass. Katie was the only woman he'd ever loved. No. There had been one other woman. A long time ago. But she'd abandoned him.

Matt flipped the blinker to turn into his driveway. Funny. Katie abandoned him through death; the other woman had abandoned him by choice. Maybe he was destined to be alone. Losing Katie had shredded his soul. He would never, ever love again. The risk was too great.

Shelby felt like a new person. Almost. Gramma had settled her into her old room on the east side of the house. The wide bay window faced the twin house next door but also afforded a view of the woods out back. This room hadn't changed either. The same white curtains graced the window; the lavender bedspread was more faded but still thick and soft. And at the edge of the window sat her favorite chair, the green-and-white shell back with a tufted ottoman to prop your feet on. For the first time in years, Shelby knew a sense of belonging.

But it was temporary. Only until she could get back on her feet physically. She tried not to think about what effect heart disease might have on her future job search. Would anyone hire her with a preexisting condition? Removing her laptop from its case, she scooped up her smart phone from the nightstand and headed downstairs. She'd worry about that later.

Gramma was looking through cabinets when Shelby stepped into the kitchen. She turned and frowned at the devices in Shelby's hands. "What are you going to do with those?"

"I have a few loose ends to tie up at work. I'm still employed for the moment, and the magazine has to go on. Medical leave or not." Truth was, there was little she could do. Everything was on hold, but it helped to keep busy. It made her feel like she was doing something.

Ellen planted her fists on her hips and pursed her lips. "You're supposed to be relaxing, and if you have any sense at all, you'll follow orders. You'll unplug yourself from those things and you'll rest, eat right and get some exercise."

She acknowledged the necessity of following the doctor's advice, but *Tween Scene* was her baby, and she'd spent every ounce of her time and energy over the years making it successful. To suddenly turn her back and walk away when its future was in doubt seemed irresponsible. Besides, what was she supposed to do with her time? Sit in the rocker and crochet?

"I'm not good at being idle, Gramma."

"Resting and taking care of yourself is not being idle."

"You know what I mean." Shelby placed her computer on the kitchen table. "I need to be busy. You know how Mom felt about being unproductive. If she had any idea how much time I spent looking at your magazines when I was here, she'd have never let me come back."

"Your mother wanted you to have an education and be able to take care of yourself."

"And I can, but now everyone's telling me to stop and stand still."

Gramma exhaled a sympathetic sigh. "I understand. But this is a new chapter in your life, and you'll have to find something different to fill your time. Something quieter, slower paced."

The thought made Shelby's skin crawl. She didn't like being inactive. She like planning and deadlines. "I'm not sure I can do that."

"You don't really have a choice." Gramma patted her shoulder. "I'm sorry to go off and leave you on your first day home, but I'm filling in at the hospital this afternoon for a friend. There's chicken salad in the fridge in case you get hungry. It's made with all low-fat, healthy ingredients. I'll be home in a couple of hours if you want to eat together. In the meantime, relax."

An hour later Shelby tossed her cell phone onto the dining room table and buried her head in her hands. It looked like the other shoe was about to drop at Harmon Publishing. Her boss had called to tell her a meeting had been scheduled for all upper management regarding the sale, but no other information had been given.

The ever-present knot of anxiety in her stomach grew. What would she do if she lost her job? How would she survive? Her mind churned with a frightening list of possible disasters. Her heart rate quickened, and a steady pressure began to build in her chest. She closed her eyes against a wave of fear. Was she having another heart attack or an anxiety attack? The doctor said the symptoms were similar. She'd been oblivious to her first episode, so how did she know if this was serious or not?

"Please, Lord, don't let this be another one." She'd experienced these symptoms before—the light-headedness, then a clammy sensation and a strange sense of foreboding. Her first thought had been a brain tumor. When the symptoms persisted, she'd gone to the clinic, but they'd sent her home with instructions to cut back on caffeine and sugar.

A second episode sent her to the hospital, where extensive tests had been run. That's when Dr. Morgan had delivered his diagnosis and his ultimatum. Time off or face the consequences. She couldn't afford to ignore this any longer. Not when death was the option.

Inhaling a slow, deep breath, she breathed a sigh of relief when her pulse slowed to normal once again and the tension eased. Frustration and anger quickly took its place, driving her outside onto the wooden porch swing. Her favorite refuge. The gentle back-and-forth movement settled her thoughts. It wasn't fair. All she'd ever wanted was to work for a magazine. Her whole life since high school had been geared toward her career. She'd studied hard and sacrificed much to achieve her goal. Now it was all being taken away. Why was God doing this to her? Was this her punishment for ignoring Him all this time?

Tears stung the backs of her eyes. She squeezed them shut, unwilling to give in. She never cried. But since her diagnosis she'd started bursting into tears at the drop of a hat. It was infuriating.

"Chester!"

She looked up at the shout to see a small, scruffy gray dog dart up the steps of the porch and stop at her feet. The little dog growled and barked, inching forward then back as he defended his territory.

Shelby chuckled softly. "Oh, hush. I'm not going to hurt you." Slowly she opened her hand, palm up, and inched it toward the dog. "See, it's okay."

The dog stopped growling and studied her. He retreated, then cocked his head and slowly moved forward. "There. Nothing to be upset about." The dog's tail began to wag furiously and he licked her hand. "Good doggie." She stroked his small head. It was soft and warm.

"Chester! You'd better get yourself back over here before you get in trouble."

Shelby looked up as a young girl came toward the house from the driveway. She appeared to be about eleven years old.

"Chester!" She hurried up the steps, placing her hands on her waist when she saw the dog. "You are in big trouble, mister." She glanced at Shelby. "I'm sorry he barked at you, ma'am."

"That's okay. I think we worked it out. He's a good watchdog. He knew I was a stranger so he was probably trying to protect you."

The girl shrugged. "I guess." She studied Shelby intently for a long moment. "Does Mrs. Bower know you're here?"

Shelby smiled. "Yes. I'm going to be staying here for a while. I'm her granddaughter."

The girl frowned. "I don't remember you."

"I've been away a long time. I live in New York City." Shelby swallowed the regret that had been nagging at her since coming home. "My name is Shelby. And I take it this is Chester?"

"Yeah," she groaned in disgust and frowned. "I didn't name him. My brother did. My name is Cassidy."

Shelby couldn't help but smile at her grown-up indignation. "Nice to meet you, Cassidy." Footsteps sounded on the steps, and a little boy joined them. He was out of breath.

"Aw, Chester you are in tra-bull. You can't come over here."

Cassidy rolled her eyes. "This is my little brother, Kenny. He's six."

Kenny stared at her.

"I'm Shelby. I'm staying here with my grandmother, Mrs. Bower."

"Oh." He smiled, displaying two deep dimples at the sides of his mouth. "She makes us sugar cookies."

"I know. She made them for me when I was little. In fact, she made some for me today. Would you like one?"

Cassidy took hold of Chester's collar. "Thanks, but we can't take food from strangers."

Shelby was momentarily taken aback. Then common sense kicked in and she smiled at the children. "That's a good rule. You're right. Maybe after we get to know each other, we can share some cookies."

Cassidy smiled. Her thickly lashed, dark blue eyes triggered something familiar in the back of Shelby's mind, but she couldn't place it.

"We have to take Chester home now." Cassidy tugged the dog toward the steps. "Our aunt will be wondering where we are."

"Okay. Nice to have met you. You and Chester are welcome here any time."

"Thanks. I'll tell my dad." Cassidy waved goodbye.

Shelby stood and walked to the edge of the porch, watching the children tugging the little dog back home. She'd wondered who lived next door in the duplicate house. Gramma had told her Mrs. Marshall had passed away several years ago and the house had changed hands a couple of times. Obviously a family lived there now.

As the children neared the porch of their home, an old battered van pulled into the driveway. The sign painted on the side read "Handy Works." Decals of various tools decorated the side panels, proclaiming some sort of handyman business.

Shelby watched as the children hurried toward the van. The door opened, and a man emerged. Tall and well-built with dark brown hair, the deep blue knit shirt he wore emphasized strong, broad shoulders and muscular arms. Faded, well-worn jeans hugged his long legs like an old friend. Dusty, work-scuffed Western boots completed the masculine picture.

He turned, arms open as the children ran to him. He lifted them off the ground in a tight hug, swinging them back and forth playfully. Shelby smiled. Not only was the man ridiculously attractive, he obviously adored his children. A lethal combination. Cassidy and Kenny began chatting away. She could hear their little voices across the wide, shared driveway. Kenny suddenly pointed toward her, and she smiled, raising her hand. The father turned and faced her. Her heart froze. Blood drained from her face.

No. It couldn't be. *Please, Lord, don't do this to me.* The man staring back at her was the last man on earth she wanted to see. Cassidy and Kenny's father was Matthias Durrant, the fiancé she'd jilted for her career fifteen years ago.

Chapter Two

Matt Durrant turned his back and followed his children into the house, his jaw clenched, his gut in knots.

Shelby was back.

He never expected to see her in Dover again. Ever. She'd made her opinion of small-town life abundantly clear the day she gave back his ring. *"I don't want a small-town man with small-town dreams."*

Shelby Russell had broken his heart and abandoned him when he'd needed her most. He'd counted on her love and support to sustain him through a difficult time in his life. But instead she'd cut and run, giving back his ring, accusing him of breaking his promise. But what about her promise to him? Her own future had been more important than their future together. He'd finally come to terms with her rejection, though he'd never understood her sudden change of heart. Never understood how she could claim to love him one minute and walk away the next. It was only several years later, when he'd met Katie, that he'd been able to put Shelby's rejection behind him and move forward.

So why, after all this time, did his heart still sting from Shelby's rejection? And why had that brief glimpse of her hit him like a lightning bolt, filling his mind with things he thought he'd forgotten? He remembered her brown eyes had small specks of gold in them. He remembered the silken feel of her long brown hair, now worn shoulder-length and soft around her face. He remembered the impish, self-conscious smile that would make his heart skip a beat.

The girlish figure he remembered had given way to soft, womanly curves. Maturity looked good on her. He hated himself for noticing. He hated more that she could still cause a reaction in him after all this time. After what she'd done.

"Daddy, she was really nice." Cassidy's blue eyes were bright with excitement. "And she's from New York."

Matt frowned. He'd been bombarded with his children's disjointed conversation from the moment he'd climbed from the van. Something about a lady and cookies. When he glanced over at the house it had all become clear. He rubbed his forehead in irritation. "How did you meet her?"

"I told you," Cassidy explained, her tone tinged with irritation. "When Chester ran over to her house. She was sitting on the swing, and Chester was barking. I guess he thought she was a stranger so he was trying to warn us. Only she wasn't a stranger. She's Miss Ellen's granddaughter and then—"

Matt placed a hand on his daughter's shoulder. "Okay. I get the picture."

Cassidy smiled. "She's nice."

Matt set his jaw. That's not how he'd describe Shelby Russell. Self-centered. Insensitive. Career-driven, yes. But nice?

"She was going to give us sugar cookies, but Cassidy said no 'cause she was a stranger," Kenny complained.

"Who's a stranger?"

Matt glanced over at his younger sister, Laura Durrant, who had come to stand at the boy's side. She'd been watching the children after school each day. He had a full schedule of classes this semester, which meant he wouldn't get home until supper time. But she'd informed him two days ago that he'd have to find someone else. "That was the right thing to do, son."

Kenny's shoulders slacked. "Yes, sir, but Mrs. Bower made them. You always let us have her cookies. How come we couldn't have any this time?"

"Because you didn't know Shelby, that's why." Matt struggled to maintain his patience.

Laura frowned. "Shelby Russell?"

Matt jammed his hands into his pockets. "She's back. She's staying with Ellen Bower."

"Oh. I'll bet Miss Ellen is excited. Shelby hasn't been home since you two broke up, has she?"

"I wouldn't know." He could see his little sister's mind digesting the news.

"Hmm. Wonder what brought her back to Dover after all this time?" She glanced at him sideways, an ornery smirk on her face. "Maybe she came to look up old friends and acquaintances."

Matt forced a smile over clenched teeth. "Why don't you ask her?"

Laura raised her eyebrows and tilted her head. "I think I might. You know, I heard she's an editor at some big magazine in New York. Mom ran across her name in an article someplace. Looks like our Shelby has reached the top of the career ladder. Good for her. It's what she always wanted."

"It's *all* she ever wanted," Matt muttered softly.

Laura winced. "Is that the sound of sour grapes being trampled? You know—" she pointed a finger at her brother "—they say you never forget your first love. Well, kids, I'm out of here." She gave Cassidy a hug and Kenny a fist bump.

"You want to stay and eat?" Matt offered the invite as she moved to the door.

She winked. "Not this time. I'm booked for the evening. Oh." Laura turned back to her brother. "Have you found someone to watch the kids yet? I hate that I had to bail on you so suddenly, but I couldn't turn down the restoration job in Mobile. It'll be a huge boost to my company."

"Don't worry about it. But to answer your question, no, I haven't found anyone yet." Matt ran a hand down the back of his neck. "Normally, I'd ask Mom, but since she's running for city council, she doesn't have the time."

"What about Ellen Bower? Doesn't she watch them for you sometimes?"

"Yes, but she's so busy with her volunteer work I rarely see her. Besides, watching the kids for a short time now and again is different from watching them every day. It might be too much for her."

Laura picked up her backpack, fishing out her truck keys. "Well, you could always ask Shelby. She's right next door."

Matt gritted his teeth and followed his sister to the door. "Yeah, but for how long? She'll probably be gone before you can blink."

Laura turned to face him. "What's bothering you, big brother?"

"Nothing. Forget it." Matt smiled at his baby sister.

Looking at her, no one would ever guess the slim, pe-
tite woman was a skilled and licensed carpenter and
builder. Her company specialized in restoring old homes
and buildings. Laura couldn't stand to see anything ne-
glected and ignored.

Outside on the front porch, they both looked over at
Ellen Bower's house.

Laura, glanced sideways at her brother. "So. Are you
going to go say hello?"

"Why?"

Laura shrugged. "She's right next door. Aren't you
the least bit curious why she came back after all this
time?"

"No."

"You're going to act like she isn't there?"

He glared in response. It sounded like a good idea
to him.

Laura hoisted her backpack onto her shoulder.
"You're being childish." She turned and started down
the front steps to her truck.

Matt stood on the porch after Laura drove off, staring at the Bower house. Why was Shelby back, and
how long was she staying? She'd made it clear long
ago that she had no interest in small-town dreams. He'd
known Ellen was Shelby's grandmother, but the subject of Shelby had never come up. Besides, the likelihood of her showing up in Dover was not great—or so
he'd believed.

"Daddy, can we have mac and cheese for supper?"

Matt glanced down at his son's face, and the eager
smile chased away his concerns. "I think your aunt
Laura left us some chicken and noodles. How does that
sound?"

"With biscuits? Yum." Kenny turned and raced back

into the house, shouting the news to his sister. Matt took one last glance at the house next door and followed his son inside. He had more important things to worry about than Shelby Russell's presence in Dover. Like who was he going to get to watch his kids for the next several weeks?

Matt barely heard what his children said as he prepared the evening meal. He was too distracted by the search for a babysitter to pay much attention. He'd made a few calls to women he knew at church and the mothers of a couple of Cassidy's friends, but no one was available long-term. By the time he sat down at the table he was nearing desperation. He glanced down at his empty plate. He had no idea if the meal had been good or not.

"Can Chester sleep with me tonight?"

"No, Kenny, he can't. You know the rules." Matt rose from the table and carried his plate to the sink. He had only one option. Ellen Bower. If she turned him down, he'd be forced to look into a professional child-care service. Not something he felt comfortable doing.

"Okay, you two. Time to clean up the kitchen."

"Daddy, now that we know that lady, can I have cookies if she asks?"

Matt gritted his teeth. He didn't want his kids getting too chummy with Shelby. But then, he probably didn't need to worry. Whatever her reason for coming home, Dover couldn't hold her attention for long. She'd run back to her all-important career after a few days.

"I guess that would be all right. But I'm sure Miss Russell will be very busy. You probably won't see her much."

Kenny frowned. "But I like her. She likes Chester." He bent down and hugged the dog's neck.

Matt exhaled a huff of irritation. His son liked

Shelby. It must be some sort of weird gene in the Durrant family that drew them to her. His father and brother had liked her, too. Fifteen years ago, Matt had been engaged to her. For twenty-four hours.

"Okay, kids, finish up your chores and then you can watch television while I run next door for a few minutes."

"Are you going to say hello to Miss Shelby?" Cassidy's smile reflected her delight.

"No. I have to see if Miss Ellen can watch you after school from now on."

Cassidy emptied her glass into the sink. "Why can't Aunt Laura stay with us?"

"She's going to be working out of town." Matt pointed at Kenny. "You make sure you feed Chester and give him fresh water."

Matt made his way to the front door, mentally battling with his emotions. It would be easy to pick up the phone, call Ellen and avoid seeing Shelby. But his little sister was right about one thing. Trying to ignore Shelby, act like she wasn't right next door, was childish.

A small voice inside warned him about being near Shelby. She'd always had a powerful effect on him. She'd made him feel strong and protective. He shoved the thought aside. He was a grown man. Not a lovesick college kid.

He'd speak to Ellen, acknowledge Shelby's presence then come home. Besides, this wasn't about him. He had to protect his kids. His children had spent only a few minutes with her and she'd already cast her spell over them. With Shelby right next door, his kids would likely grow deeply attached, and then what would happen when she skipped town without warning? Broken hearts, that's what. He couldn't let that happen. She needed to understand how emotionally vulnerable Kenny and Cassidy were since their mother's death. All he was asking was that she keep her distance for the few days she was here. It wasn't an unreasonable request. Merely a "good fences make good neighbors" conversation. Setting some boundaries. That's all.

Cassidy stuck her head out the front door. "Will you tell Miss Shelby I said hi?"

Matt nodded and set his jaw. Okay, maybe a wall instead of a fence. "Will do."

Shelby closed her laptop with a firm snap and shoved away from the dining room table. Trying to work was useless. She couldn't get Matt's image out of her mind. She'd stood on the porch earlier immobilized, watching as Matt turned his back and walked away. His message loud and clear. They had nothing to say to one another.

Her insides burned with the rejection. What had she expected? That he'd be glad to see her? She'd run out on him. Told him he wasn't good enough. Her conscience stung when she remembered her cruel words to him that night. She had been so arrogant, so disdainful of what she perceived as his lack of ambition. How could she make him understand that breaking their engagement was the hardest thing she'd ever done? But he was the one who had reneged on all their dreams. She'd had no choice.

She stood and went to the kitchen and searched for something to munch. A bowl of apples sat on the counter. Common sense told her to eat one. A healthy choice. What she wanted was chocolate.

Closing her eyes, she fought the urge to look out the window at Matt's house, hungry for another glimpse of him. He was even more handsome than she'd remembered. Age had broadened his shoulders, deepened his chest and chiseled the planes of his face. There was a masculine confidence in his bearing that couldn't be ignored. And the gentle, tender heart she'd fallen in love with was displayed in the unabashed love of his children.

Matt had been everything she'd ever wanted in a man.

She opened her eyes, staring across the drive. Part of her longed to see him coming toward the house to— what? Say all was forgiven? Let's start over? But another part of her hoped he would stay on his side of the driveway and ignore her for the remainder of her stay. Confronting him would be too painful, no matter the outcome.

Her conscience stung again. Gramma was right. Avoiding conflict was one of her biggest faults. She was avoiding her illness, avoiding making the changes she needed. And now, hoping to avoid Matt.

Forcing herself to move, Shelby picked up an apple and took a bite, her mind bursting with questions. How had he come to live next door, and what had he been doing all these years? Obviously he'd married and had children. What was his wife like? Was it someone she knew from school? What about the Handy Works van? Was that what he did for a living? It would make sense. His father owned the hardware store where they'd met. She had noticed a large pickup in the drive as well, but it was gone now. Apparently he'd followed in his father's footsteps.

Movement outside the window caught her attention. She froze. Matt. He was coming over. "No. Not now. I'm not ready. I can't deal with this right now." She held her breath, watching him come across the drive.

She could still see the young man she remembered in his slow, easy gait. The male grace he'd displayed as a young man was still evident. The years had done little to diminish his attractiveness. She turned away, her stomach in knots, flinching when the knock on the door echoed through the house. He was coming to demand an answer for her breaking their engagement. What would she say? *I ran because I was afraid I'd never get out of this place if I didn't?*

Taking a deep breath, she opened the door and lost her breath. He didn't look like the father of two. With his square-jawed good looks and athletic physique, he could have graced the cover of any magazine. His dark brown hair still lay in waves across his head. The cobalt-blue eyes with their thick lashes were still compelling and magnetic. The only thing missing was his smile. She doubted if she'd ever see that again. She cleared her throat, searching desperately for her voice.

"Hello, Shelby."

"Hey." It was all she could squeak out past the lump in her throat.

Shelby motioned him inside. He nodded and stepped over the threshold. She closed the door behind him, struggling to maintain a casual attitude while ignoring the tantalizing smell of his aftershave.

"I had no idea you lived next door." She forced a smile. "It was a surprise seeing you drive up today."

Matt frowned. "Ellen didn't tell you?"

"No, but then she never knew we…" She faltered. "Gramma and Grandpa were on a mission trip the summer we dated."

He nodded, shoving his hands into his pockets.

Her heart pounded so fiercely she wondered if he

could hear it. Now that he was here, all she wanted was to get it over with. "Would you like to sit down?"

"No. I need to talk to Ellen. Is she here?"

Shelby's tension deflated like a punctured balloon. Matt wasn't here to see her at all. She should have been relieved, but instead she swallowed a large gulp of disappointment. "She's not here at the moment, but I expect her home anytime. You're welcome to wait."

Matt's jaw worked side to side a moment, as if gauging his next words.

"How long are you staying?"

She blinked. That wasn't the question she'd anticipated. Apparently he was going to get right to the point. Fine. She could take it. Raising her chin, she crossed her arms over her chest and faced him. Matt's blue gaze pierced through her. Blue eyes exactly like Cassidy's. Now she knew why they'd seemed so familiar. "Six weeks or so. My schedule is flexible."

Matt planted his hands on his hips. A smirk curved one corner of his mouth upward. "Six whole weeks. You sure you won't get bored so far from the big city? We pull in the sidewalk around seven, remember?"

"Yes. I remember." Her heart burned. He was throwing her words from long ago back in her face.

"I'm sure you do. So, what brings you back to the small-town life?"

She ignored the flash of pain his sarcasm inflicted. "I had time accrued that I needed to use, and I wanted to spend time with Gramma."

"Can the corporate world survive without you?"

She lifted her chin. He was really getting under her skin with his sour attitude. "It's the wireless age, Matt. I can do my work from anywhere. Have laptop will travel. Clouds and smart phones are our friends. You do have those things here in your small town, don't you?"

"I know all about working from home."

"Really? So the world of hammers and nails is high tech now?" Her condescending words sent a hot rush of remorse along her nerves. She hadn't meant to handle their meeting this way, as if she were eighteen and scared and confused. She'd wanted to face him as a highly successful, competent woman of the world.

"I don't work at the store anymore, Shelby. That's my father's job."

There was a low, threatening undercurrent to his tone that scraped against her nerves. She ignored it. "So you have your own handyman business now? I saw the van when you drove up."

Matt's eyes darkened, and he shifted his weight slightly as if trying to control himself. "I only do that part-time. You know how we small-town guys are. We work as little as possible so we have more time to hunt and fish. We're not very ambitious."

Shelby cringed at hearing her own words taunting her. So much for putting on a front. Being face-to-face with him hurt more than she'd ever imagined. "Matt, please…"

The sound of a car pulling in the drive meant Gramma was back. Her chance to escape. "I'll let Gramma know you're here." Quickly she moved through the hall and into the kitchen, meeting Ellen as she opened the door. "Why didn't you tell me Matt Durrant lived next door to you?"

Ellen blinked in surprise. "I didn't think you'd care."

"I don't. I mean, it was a surprise, that's all."

Gramma came into the kitchen, a puzzled frown

marring her brow. "What difference could that make to you?"

"Because we were—" She hesitated, gauging her words. "We knew each other in school."

Gramma shook her head. "I don't understand. What does that have to do with anything?"

Shelby exhaled an exasperated grunt. There was no way she could make Gramma understand without going into the grim details of her past relationship with Matt, and she wasn't ready to deal with that right now. "Never mind. He's here. He wants to talk to you."

"Well, why didn't you say so?" Gramma set her purse and a small sack of groceries on the counter, then strode toward the living room. Shelby followed slowly behind, stopping at the archway and leaning against the side. The more distance between her and Matt the better.

"Hello, Matt. You wanted to talk to me?"

Shelby listened as Matt quickly outlined the situation. Apparently he was in dire need of a babysitter. Something about all-day classes and needing help after school. What that had to do with a handyman business she didn't know. She had to wonder where the mother was. Out of town perhaps?

"Oh dear, I don't know. I'm so busy with my church work and the hospital. I hate to turn you down but..." Ellen turned to Shelby and smiled. "I have it. Shelby and I can both watch them. We'll be like a tag team. When I'm volunteering she can fill in. It's the perfect solution."

Shelby couldn't believe her ears. It took her a full second to find her voice. "What? No. I can't. I mean—" She glanced over at Matt, who looked as horrified by the idea as she did.

"No. I mean, I wouldn't dream of imposing on your

granddaughter while she's visiting. I'm sure I can work something out."

Ellen waved off his concerns. "What are neighbors for? When do we start?"

Matt shifted his weight. "Tomorrow afternoon, but…" Gramma's landline suddenly rang, breaking the tension in the room. "Oh, I'd better get that. That'll be fine, Matt. I'm free in the afternoon. Send the children over here when they get off the bus." Ellen waved at Matt and hurried toward the other room, leaving Shelby alone with Matt again.

Shelby searched for something to say. "Matt, I—"

"You met my kids." His tone was flat and cool.

Shelby nodded, mentally scurrying to regain her footing at his abrupt change of subject. "They're adorable. I like their dog, too." She couldn't help but smile at the thought of them. "They were very well-behaved. Cassidy politely refused my offer of cookies because she didn't know me. You and your wife should be proud. You've done a wonderful job with them."

Matt paled. His eyes turned dark and cold. "My wife died three years ago."

She gasped. "Oh, Matt. I didn't know. I'm so sorry." He pinned her with a cold blue glare.

"My kids have been through a lot. They're emotionally vulnerable and they tend to give their hearts too easily. I don't want those hearts broken by a stranger passing through town."

Stranger? Was that how he thought of her now? Before she could respond, he turned and walked to the door.

He stopped, looking over his shoulder. "Do we understand each other?"

There was a warning in his tone that was impossible to miss—*stay away from my children.* She nodded, stunned and dazed. The door closed behind him with a sharp pop, like a bullet to her heart.

Matt strode across the driveway. He shouldn't have gone to Ellen's. He should have called. He thought he'd been prepared to face Shelby again, but he'd been wrong. From the moment she'd opened the door he'd been rattled. She looked even more amazing up close, as fresh and lovely as he'd remembered. Her nearness had released a kaleidoscope of memories he didn't want to explore. There was so much he'd wanted to say, to ask, but nothing would change the past. Nothing would explain away the wound she'd inflicted.

At the edge of the driveway, he stopped, casting his eyes upward briefly. Ellen's solution to his babysitting problem had blindsided him. He had wanted to turn her down flat, shout that he didn't want Shelby close to his kids. The last thing he needed was for his kids to form an attachment to Shelby, because when she left, and she would leave, the kids would lose another close relationship. He wouldn't let that happen. But he'd been trapped. Ellen was his only option.

If only Katie were here. She'd know how to handle this. But if she were, there would be no need. He'd have his wife back, his kids would have their mom and he wouldn't feel like he was constantly treading water just to survive.

As he walked past the Handy Works van, the words written on the side panel caught his attention. *Showing God's Grace.* He stopped. Remorse surged through him. He hadn't shown any grace to Shelby just now. He'd been curt, rude and unfeeling. Not the way he'd intended it to go. Or was it?

His conscience faulted him for being harsh and judgmental, but his heart told him he had to protect his kids from people like Shelby. People who turned their backs on the things in life that really mattered. He owed her an apology for his bad attitude but not for his position. As far as he was concerned, she was a stranger passing through. Nothing more.

Matt set his jaw and strode past the van toward the house. Shelby had assumed he had a handyman business. He should have expected that. She'd called him "a small-town man with small-town dreams." He'd started to explain, then changed his mind. Let her believe whatever she wanted.

All that mattered was protecting the hearts of his children.

Shelby stared at the closed door, struggling to breathe through the thickness in her throat. She'd imagined her reunion with Matt in a thousand different ways, but never like that. She knew she'd hurt him when she'd broken their brief engagement, and she'd expected him to be angry. But the man who had walked out of the house wasn't the gentle, tender boy she remembered. He was a fierce, protective guardian warning her to keep her distance from his children.

He'd made his opinion of her crystal clear. He had never forgiven her for what she'd done. She couldn't blame him. She'd turned her back on everything he cared about. Belittled his beliefs and his dreams. She sank into a kitchen chair, fighting tears. "Small-town man with small-town dreams."

How many times had she longed to take back her angry words? She wanted to explain to him how she'd felt that night fifteen years ago. How scared and confused she'd been. They'd had plans to go to college, to escape the backward life of Dover. But the day after he'd given her the ring, he'd changed. Instead of talking about their dreams for the future, he'd talked about settling down, staying in Dover. She'd felt betrayed. He'd said he wanted the same things she did, but apparently a ring on her finger had erased all that. Her mother's dire warning was coming true. She'd said that ring only meant one thing, that Matt would expect her to give up her dreams for his. "You'll be trapped here just like me." She hadn't wanted to believe her mother was right, but at that moment, it had seemed all too true.

It had all been so clear to her then. Either marry Matt and spend the rest of her life in a choked-off life in Mississippi or run like crazy toward college and her dreams of working on a magazine. Only one course of action had made sense. Run. It had been a matter of survival. And she'd achieved her dream. She stood at the top of her field. Though for how much longer, she didn't know.

But at the moment she had a more urgent concern. Gramma was setting the table when she entered the kitchen. "Gramma, I can't babysit Matt's kids."

"You aren't, sweetie. I am. You'll be my backup. It'll be fun. They are darling kids. You'll love them."

"I met them this afternoon while you were gone. Their dog came over."

"Aren't they precious?" Gramma smiled. "Matt and Katie did a great job."

Katie. The wife. Her throat tightened. "How did his wife die?"

"Cancer. That's why he moved back home."

Back home? "He hasn't been here the whole time?"

"No. He owned some kind of big computer business

in Atlanta. He sold it and moved back here about a year ago to be closer to his family."

Shelby sorted through this new information. She'd always assumed Matt would never leave Dover. It was the crux of their breakup. It didn't make sense.

Sinking down into the chair, she rested her elbows on the table and cradled her aching head. Could things get any worse? She'd come here to rest, ease the stress in her life, but how was she supposed to do that with Matt right next door? She'd have been better off if she'd stayed in New York. Matt's pointed warning echoed in her mind. "He doesn't want me watching his kids, Gramma."

Ellen set the plates down on the table, a deep frown creasing her forehead. "Is there something between you two I should know about?"

Shelby inhaled. Great. She couldn't avoid this any longer. "We dated." Might as well tell it all. "We were engaged. Briefly. We broke up." She hoped her grandmother wouldn't press for more details. She couldn't deal with that at the moment.

"I see. When was this?"

"The summer before I went to college. I was working at the Durrant's hardware store. You and Grandpa were in Belize." She shrugged as if it were insignificant, hoping her grandmother would let the subject drop.

"Oh." Gramma lowered herself onto a chair. "I had no idea you were serious about anyone. That does make things awkward, but that was a long time ago. Why should it bother you so much now? Unless…" Gramma eyed her closely. "Ah. I see."

Shelby squirmed. She never could hide her feelings from her grandmother.

"Well, it seems to me you two need to settle this thing between you pretty quick. It's been going on way too long, don't you agree?"

Chapter Three

Matt closed the lid on the Insect Man lunch box and set it beside the matching backpack. A quick glance around the kitchen revealed an escaped homework folder peeking out from under the stack of mail and flyers for his mom's city council campaign. He pulled it out and unzipped Cassidy's pink plaid backpack, sliding the folder inside as he called her name. "Cassidy. It's time to go. Hurry it up, please."

Kenny skidded to a halt beside the kitchen island, holding up his hands and baring his teeth for inspection. Matt turned the little palms over, then tilted his son's face upward. "Looking good, sport."

Kenny smiled and reached for his backpack. "Do we still get to go to Miss Ellen's after school?"

Matt masked his concern with a forced smile. "Yes. And I expect you to behave yourselves."

"Will Miss Shelby be there?" Cassidy slung her backpack over her shoulder and looked at him with expectant eyes. He stared down at her. Something was different. Her hair was sticking out on one side. He'd learned the hard way not to question his daughter's fashion sense too vigorously. Maybe she meant it to look like that. "Uh, I suppose. But I'm sure she'll be busy with her work, so don't bother her. Miss Ellen is your babysitter." And if he could make other arrangements he would. He wanted as much separation between Shelby Russell and his kids as possible.

"Okay, everyone to the van. We're running out of time."

Kenny's eyes widened. "You mean we get to ride to school in the Handy Works van?"

"'Fraid so. I left my car at Grandpa's store yesterday."

Cassidy's shoulders sagged, and she exhaled a disgusted whine. "Can't we go get our car first? The van is ugly."

"Ugly or not, it's your only mode of transportation this morning." Matt touched her shoulder, steering her toward the door.

"At least I'll get to see Miss Shelby when I get home."

Matt groaned inwardly. He had no choice about babysitters for the next couple of days, but he fully intended to beat every bush and look behind every tree until he found someone else to watch his kids.

Pulling the door closed behind him, Matt followed his kids to the van. Confident in his plan.

Shelby stared out the kitchen window at Matt's house. She'd been forced to alter her assumptions about him. Not only had Matt left Dover, but he'd had a successful business and a wonderful marriage. Losing his wife had wounded him deeply. The grief reflected in his eyes still haunted her. As did his very pointed warning.

Did Matt think she would deliberately hurt his kids? Probably. He was assuming that she would walk out on them the way she had him. He wasn't going to forgive her, and she had no one to blame but herself. She was finally reaping what she had sown.

So how was she supposed to babysit and still keep her distance? Hopefully, most of the babysitting duties would fall to Gramma and she'd keep a very low profile for the next few weeks.

The mantel clock in the living room struck the half hour, jerking Shelby rudely from her computer screen. Two-thirty. She'd worked through lunch, and now Cassidy and Kenny were due home soon and Gramma wasn't home yet. A rush of anxiety warmed her blood. Where was she? After dialing Ellen's cell number, Shelby waited impatiently. No answer. She tried again a few minutes later with the same result. This was not good.

Shelby paced the living room, her gaze darting through the front window to the end of the driveway. Matt would not be happy if she ended up being the babysitter today. With a nervous sigh Shelby stepped out onto the front porch and stood at the edge of the steps. There was nothing she could do but make sure Matt's kids were safe and sound when he came home. How hard could that be? She really liked his kids. She'd lost her heart to them the moment she'd met them. If it wasn't for his staunch disapproval of her, she'd be looking forward to spending time with them.

The low rumble of a diesel engine sounded in the distance. Shelby moved down the porch steps to the sidewalk, watching as the big yellow bus stopped and opened its doors. Kenny was off first, his little legs breaking into a run that sent his backpack bobbing up and down. He waved, a huge happy smile on his face as he raced toward her.

"Hi. I beat Cass. She walks too slow."

Shelby laughed out loud. She was shocked to realize it had been a very long time since she'd known any true joy. The bus pulled away, and Shelby watched as Cassidy waved to someone then started toward her.

"Hi. I'm glad you're going to watch us."

The child's comment sent a rush of warmth through Shelby's heart. "Me, too. I'm looking forward to spending time with both of you." It was the truth. Whatever problems Matt had, whatever reservations he held, he'd have to handle on his own. She wasn't going to close herself off from these adorable children just because he harbored an old grudge.

"Miss Ellen left you some cookies. Are you hungry?" The responses were unanimous. Shelby followed the energetic kids up the steps and into the house. For the next three hours she was going to enjoy herself. Matt Durrant could just deal with it.

Matt pulled into the driveway, parking his car close to the side door of the house. His tension eased when he saw Ellen's car parked in its normal spot. He'd managed to get off work early. He hadn't been comfortable with the kids being around Shelby. He asked around the campus but found no alternative child care. He'd even called the local nanny service, but the cost was ridiculous. Hopefully he'd be able to make different arrangements over the weekend. His kids were still fragile emotionally. He had to make sure they were protected.

A firm tap on Ellen's front door brought no response. Ellen rarely locked her door, so he tapped again then eased it open. He smiled when he recognized his children's laughter. "Hello, anybody here? It's me."

"Daddy's home!" Kenny's shout echoed through the house. Matt stepped into the foyer in time to catch his son as he propelled himself up into his arms. "Hey, sport. Sounds like you're having a good time."

Kenny nodded and let go. "We're looking at pictures of you. Come see."

"Me?" Matt followed his son into the dining room, trying to find a reason why Ellen would have pictures of him. Cassidy was seated at one end of the table, her chair pulled close to Shelby's. A board game was laid out on the opposite end. His daughter looked over her shoulder and smiled, sending his heart into meltdown. His little princess had him tightly wrapped around her sweet little finger.

"Hey, Daddy. Come see. We found pictures of you in high school. Look, look." She motioned him to look over her shoulder. Matt moved forward, noticing for the first time the smile on Shelby's face. Her brown eyes sparkled, highlighting the gold flecks, and there was a soft rosy glow in her cheeks. She looked contented and happy. Matt stepped to his daughter's right side, away from Shelby, but the faint flowery scent of her fragrance drifted around him.

"Look, Dad, that's you." Cassidy pointed to a picture in a yearbook. He had to smile. Had he ever looked that young? He chuckled softly deep in his throat. "That would be me, all right."

"You have lots of pictures in here."

Matt reached out and folded back the cover to check the date. His senior year. "Yeah, I was pretty active that year. How did this turn up at Ellen's house?" He directed his question to Shelby.

"It's mine. I bought one every year. I was usually on the staff, so." She shrugged. "I kept a lot of my things here at Gramma's. We didn't have much room in our apartment, and my mom liked to throw things out."

"So where's Ellen? I assumed she'd be here." He felt like a heel when Shelby blanched at his question. But he'd arranged for her grandmother to watch the kids. Not her.

"She's next door. Mrs. Horvath is under the weather, and she took her a casserole."

Kenny had climbed back into his chair on the other side of his sister. "Daddy, is Mommy's picture in the book?"

Matt braced against the pain the simple question stirred up. Would it always be this way? "No, son. Your mom didn't grow up in Dover."

"Where did she grow up?"

"In Savannah, Georgia. Remember, we went to the beach there right before she got sick?"

"I remember." Cassidy's happy mood had vanished.

Time to get his kids back into their own safe space. "Come on, kids. We'd better go home. You have homework, and we need to start supper."

"We did our homework first thing." Cassidy pushed back from the table.

"Dad, can we look at pictures of Mom after supper?"

"Sure, son." He turned toward the door, aware of Shelby following behind him and also aware that he had to thank her. The kids gathered up their backpacks, then clustered near him at the front door.

"Matt." He wasn't in the mood to talk to her, but he couldn't be rude. She had kept his children safe and entertained. He pulled open the door and gestured his kids to leave. "Y'all go on over to the house. I'll be along in a minute." He turned to face Shelby.

"I hope I didn't cause any trouble with the yearbooks. It never occurred to me that they'd expect to see pictures of their mother."

"Not your fault. I never know when the questions will come. They catch me off guard all the time."

"I can't image how difficult this is for you and the children. She was obviously a wonderful mother."

"She was." Sweet recollections drifted through his mind, but this time without the biting sting. "She was funny, always thinking of new ways to entertain them. She knew exactly what to say and do for any situation. Losing her traumatized the kids. Especially Cassidy. I put her in counseling for a while. She was like a lost puppy."

"Is that why you moved back home, to be around your family?"

Her question made him realize that he'd been spilling his guts to Shelby. Absolutely not what he'd intended. But then, she'd always been easy to talk to. She knew things about him no one else did. But she didn't need to know about his pain and loss. Not that she'd care. She was only passing through.

He had to remember his primary goal here. Keep his kids from any more heartbreak. "Yes. I felt they needed some stability. Some security. Atlanta was too full of memories. I sold my business and everything else and came home." He held her gaze, willing her to understand what he was about to say. "My kids have suffered deeply in losing their mother. I want them to be surrounded by people who love them as much as I do. I want them to have people in their lives they can depend on, who won't walk out when they need them most." He stopped, realizing he wasn't talking about his family anymore. He saw Shelby's brown eyes darken.

"People like *me*, Matt?"

He set his jaw. "I didn't say that."

"You didn't have to."

Matt turned to leave. "Tell Ellen thanks. I'm still looking for other babysitting options. I know she misses her volunteer work, and I don't like imposing on you."

Shelby crossed her arms over her chest. "Because I'm not dependable?"

No sense playing games. "No. You're not."

The afternoon light streamed through the windowed walls of the sunroom on the back of Gramma's house, casting a warm glow on the cozy space. Curled up in the old chaise, a magazine in her lap, she reveled in the familiar sense of peace. She glanced around the room at the stacks of magazines and smiled. She'd fallen in love with magazines because of her gramma. She'd hurry over here after school and lose herself in the glossy pages of beautiful rooms, filled with beautiful people doing beautiful things. Life within the pages was always perfect and happy. Magazines allowed her to escape her mother's bitterness and forget for a while that she didn't fit in at school.

She could almost relax completely, if it weren't for Cassidy and Kenny coming over shortly. After a quick hello yesterday, she'd escaped to her room, explaining she had work to do and leaving Gramma to watch over the kids. She'd missed being with them but it allowed her to avoid Matt. She hadn't come out of her room until she'd seen the three Durrants walking across the drive to their house.

Gramma's advice had hovered in the back of her mind. It was time to settle the past. All this huffing and puffing was silly. But how did they do that when it was clear that Matt would never forgive her for walking out?

Today, however, she couldn't use work as an excuse to avoid babysitting. Gramma had called to say she'd been invited to dinner and a movie with friends. She wanted to know if Shelby was okay with keeping the kids. Shelby couldn't refuse. Her grandmother deserved a night out, but that left her to deal with Matt's disapproval.

She set her jaw. She was not going to worry herself into knots over this. Matt needed someone responsible to keep the kids; she was his only option. All she could do was be as conscientious as possible, and hopefully in time he'd come to trust her.

Squealing air brakes sounded outside, and she found herself smiling, even as a trickle of nervousness formed. What did she know about taking care of children? She'd certainly never learned anything from her mother. She'd always made motherhood seem like a burden, the worse choice a woman could make. But Matt's adorable kids were making her take a new look at some of her assumptions.

Shelby met the children halfway down the drive. "Hello there." Seeing their sweet, happy faces warmed her heart in a way she'd never experienced before. Cassidy fell into step with her as they made their way back toward Gramma's house. Kenny raced ahead.

"I'm glad it's Friday. No school for two whole days."

"Don't you like school?"

Cassidy nodded. "But I don't like homework."

"Join the club. No one does." Shelby glanced up at Kenny, who stood on his porch, backpack at his feet. "Kenny, come on. Gramma left some brownies today."

"Can't we stay at our house today? Please? I want to play with Chester. I don't want to wait until Dad gets home."

Cassidy nodded. "Could we? I like being at your house, but I'd really like to go home."

Shelby couldn't think of any reason not to, other than she would feel uncomfortable in Matt's home. But her primary concern was the children. "I suppose. Let me go get the key and a few of my things."

Standing in Matt's house a few minutes later, she couldn't resist the temptation to look around. Unlike her grandmother's house, which retained all its original details, Matt's home had been completely remodeled. Walls had been removed, rooms opened up and windows replaced, giving the home an open, spacious feel. Despite the clean lines and modern style, the furniture was practical and functional. Evidence of the children lay scattered around the room—toys on the floor, a stuffed animal on the ottoman. Matt's work boots stood beside the leather recliner.

She forced herself to ignore her surroundings. Quickly she moved to the kitchen and set her laptop on the table. Cassidy, never far from her side, took the brownies and set them on the island. "Any homework?"

"A little. But I can do it Sunday night."

Shelby laid an arm across the girl's shoulders. "Would you like some advice, woman to woman?" Cassidy nodded, a huge smile on her face. "Do you know what the word *procrastinate* means?"

Cassidy groaned softly. "To put stuff off."

"Yep. I learned after much painful struggle that the best way to enjoy your time off is by getting the unpleasant things out of the way first. It's freeing. I think you should try it."

Cassidy pointed to the treats on the counter.

Shelby shook her head. "Before we have brownies."

With the young girl up in her room and Kenny safely in the backyard with Chester, Shelby took a moment to check emails on her smart phone. There was no more news about the future of the company. Not surprising. Everything was on hold until the upcoming meeting. It was the not knowing that kept her on edge. The cold hard truth was the chances of her being out of work soon were very good. And she couldn't get back to New York to look for another job until she had her health back on track.

"I used to live in Atlanta when I was little," Cassidy stated as they munched on homemade brownies a short while later. Kenny had scooped his up and returned to the yard, mumbling something about finding a lizard on the fence.

Shelby was still picking at her piece, knowing she shouldn't be eating the chocolate treat but unable to completely resist. "So I heard. Atlanta is a very big city."

"There's a lot to do there. Not like here."

Shelby stifled a grin at the girls assumed air of sophistication. "Don't you like Dover?"

"It's okay. I didn't like it much when I first got here. Boring." She rolled her eyes. "But I have friends now so it's not so bad." Cassidy took another bite of brownie. "What do you do in New York?"

"I edit a magazine. You may know it. *Tween Scene.*"

Cassidy eyes widened. "Really? That's the coolest magazine ever."

"Thank you." Shelby couldn't help a swell of pride at the compliment. She'd worked hard to make the magazine a success. It broke her heart to think it might be discontinued under the new management.

"I can't believe that's your magazine. Wait until I tell my friends."

"Well, it's not mine. I don't own it. I only work for it, but I'm glad to hear you like *Tween Scene* so much. What's your favorite section?"

Cassidy thought a moment. "The one where they show you what to wear and what not to wear. And the makeup one, and the part where you talk about TV stars. Only...I'm not allowed to read it."

Shelby stopped midbite. "What? But you're so familiar with it."

"I know, but Dad says it's too grown-up for me. He says the articles aren't good for girls my age."

Tween Scene precisely targeted Cassidy's demographic. Did Matt really disapprove or was he steering her away from the publication because she was the editor? Come to think of it, did he even know she was connected to the magazine? Could his comments be solely objective? Doubtful. *Tween Scene* was perfect. "I'm sorry to hear that. We try very hard to make the magazine appeal to girls your age. If your dad won't let you read it, how do you know so much about it?"

A guilty smile moved her lips. "I read it at Molly's."

"Oh. I see."

"You won't tell Dad, will you?"

"No. But do you think you should be disobeying your father?"

Cassidy shook her head. "But it's such a cool magazine."

Cool in the young girl's eyes. Inappropriate in her parent's. Which one was the truth? As far as Shelby could recall, nothing in *Tween Scene* should cause concern in parents. Apparently, Matt's overprotective streak ran to more than just their hearts.

"I wish I was thin and pretty like you," Cassidy said, her voice soft and wistful. Shelby made a quick survey of the little girl. She wasn't rail thin, but she wasn't chubby, either. She was nicely filled out and starting to transform into a young lady. "I think you're perfect."

Cassidy smiled. "Thanks, but I want to look like that girl on the cover last time. You know, the one where she was wearing those cool jeans and that striped top with the patches."

She remembered it well. It had been one of the best covers all year. "That was Yasmine."

Shelby thought about the child models and celebrities she worked with regularly. They were nothing like Cassidy. Most were mature beyond their years and bone thin. Nearly all the models were older than the preteen image *Tween Scene* promoted. Something about that bothered her, but she wasn't sure what.

"I wish I could look like that." Cassidy sighed wistfully. "She's so cool."

Shelby could remember when she felt the same way. She'd look at the girls in the magazines and long for a magic wand that could transform her into a glamorous model.

"I have an idea." Shelby moved to the table and pulled out her smart phone and opened her laptop.

"What are we going to do?"

"You'll see." Shelby winked, opening her camera app. "I have a magic wand." She motioned Cassidy to stand against the wall. "Okay, now strike a pose."

Cassidy giggled self-consciously. "I don't know what to do."

Shelby began taking pictures. "Pretend you're a model. Pose like you see the girls on the cover of my magazine."

A few minutes later, Shelby moved to her laptop and pulled up the images. "Come watch." Cassidy came to her side. After selecting her editing program, she scrolled through the shots to find the best image to work with. First she added highlights and fullness to Cassidy's hair. Next she made her eyes larger and deepened the color, adding sparkle for good measure. A click of the mouse slimmed the neck and added hollows to the cheeks. Another whitened the teeth. One more trimmed the body line.

Lastly, she turned her attention to the clothes. She lightened the hue of the jeans and changed the color of the blouse to a jewel tone that better complemented the new deeper shade of her eyes. A few more minor touch-ups, and Shelby leaned back in her chair. "Well, what do you think?"

"Oh wow. I look like a TV star." She was breathless. "That is so cool."

Shelby gave the girl a quick hug. "You look exactly like the girls on the covers of my magazine. In fact." She made a few more clicks and added the magazine banner across the top of the page, making the picture resemble the cover of *Tween Scene*.

"It's me, but it's not me. Oh thank you, thank you," Cassidy gushed, bouncing up and down. "This is so awesome. Can I have a copy?"

"Sure. I'm not connected to your printer though. I can email it to you so you can print it out. What's your address?" Shelby typed in the address, attached the file and hit Send. "There you go. Do you know how to print on your computer?"

"We only have Dad's. He won't let us have our own. He says we're too young."

"I'm sure he'll print it for you when he gets here." She glanced at the wall clock. Matt would be home before long. "What are you doing for supper? Should I be putting something in the oven?"

Cassidy shrugged. "I don't know. Aunt Laura usually made something for us, but she's not here now."

Cassidy's eyes grew wide, and Shelby saw excitement building.

"What?"

"Can I cook supper for Daddy? I could surprise him."

It was a sweet idea. "Do you know how to cook?"

"A little. I help Aunt Laura sometimes. I know how to make lasagna. My gramma showed me how."

Shelby was warming to the idea. She used to love to cook, but like many of her favorite pastimes, she'd given it up for lack of time. "I think that's a great idea. Let's see if we have everything we need." Cassidy jumped into the task with gusto, surprising Shelby with how much she knew. Working with the little girl on the dinner and helping her through the process was a surprisingly satisfying experience.

Shelby watched the clock. Matt should be home any moment and all was ready. "Cassidy, you did a wonderful job." Even Kenny had contributed his table-setting skills. All that remained was for their dad to come home and enjoy their efforts.

Cassidy kept dashing to the front door, looking for Matt's car. "Do you think he'll be surprised? What if he doesn't like it?"

Shelby squeezed her shoulders. "He'll love it because you made if for him."

"He's here!" Kenny dashed out the back door.

Shelby's heart skipped a beat, but she didn't question the cause. This was simple pride. Her heart was bursting. She couldn't wait to see Matt's reaction. Of course then she'd slip out and go home. She had no intentions of intruding on the family meal. The feeling of disappointment over that knowledge was stronger than she'd expected. She found herself wanting to stay and be part of the camaraderie.

Matt strode through the back door, a puzzled look on his chiseled features. Kenny bounced on his feet beside him. "What's going on?" He inhaled deeply. "Something smells good."

"Cassidy did it." Kenny pointed at his sister.

Matt looked first at her then to his daughter. "Did you make dinner?"

Cassidy ran to him and wrapped her arms around his waist. "I baked lasagna. I did it all by myself."

"Miss Shelby helped, and I did, too," Kenny announced.

"I didn't know you could cook." He glanced over at Shelby.

She smiled and nodded. "She did it all by herself. I think you may have a future chef on your hands."

"Well, let's sit down and try it. I'm sure it'll taste as good as it smells." Matt's gaze met hers. "Where's Ellen?"

"She's dining out with friends." He looked like he wanted to say something then changed his mind. Had she overstepped again?

Cassidy scanned the table. "Kenny, you forgot to put a plate for Miss Shelby."

"Oh, no. I'm not staying. This is your family time."

"You have to stay. Please?" Cassidy grabbed her arm and squeezed.

She looked at Matt and cringed. Great. She'd placed Matt in an awkward position once again. Either way he replied would be uncomfortable.

"Of course she has to stay."

She looked over at Matt, gauging his expression. Was he serious or was he merely tolerating her for his daughter's sake? Suddenly she knew what she wanted to do. Lifting her chin, she met Matt's gaze. "Thank you.

I'd love to stay. I'm looking forward to having some of Cassidy's wonderful meal." He didn't flinch.

"Kenny, set another plate on the table."

The meal was more pleasant than Shelby had anticipated. Matt was sincerely impressed with his daughter's cooking efforts and Kenny kept them entertained with stories about Chester.

She'd picked at her lasagna, hoping Cassidy wouldn't notice how little she ate. As delicious as it was, the heavy pasta dish wasn't something she could indulge in.

"I'll clean up, Daddy."

Matt raised his eyebrows. "I know when to not argue. We'll be in the living room."

Reluctantly Shelby followed Matt from the room. She'd much rather be helping Cassidy with the dishes. She strived for a topic of conversation. "You have a lovely home, Matt."

"Thanks. Katie, my wife, was a decorator. She always had our home looking like a magazine spread. I have no talent in that department. I go with what I like."

"It's a very comfortable room. Very homey." Her gaze settled on a framed photo on the sofa table. She lifted it, her heart skipping a beat when she realized it was a family picture. A stately blonde smiled out at her. Katie. The wife. "She's a beautiful woman."

"Yes, she was."

The sadness in his voice broke her heart. "Kenny resembles her a good bit."

He nodded "Yes, he does. He has her personality, too. She was always busy, always involved in something. Kenny has only one speed. Fast."

"I've noticed. I wish I had some of his energy." Shelby chuckled and put the frame down. "How did you and your wife meet?"

"At school. She had a project for a design class and she needed someone good with tools to help. A friend mentioned me."

Cassidy poked her head in the room. "Daddy, I just remembered. I need to print something. Can I get on the computer?"

He moved to the desk at the end of the kitchen and tapped the keys. "There you go."

"Look, Daddy." Cassidy came to his side, holding up a picture, a beaming smile on her face. "It's me."

"You? It doesn't look anything like you." He frowned, shooting a quick glance at Shelby.

Cassidy bounced up and down, giggling with delight. "I know. Don't I look awesome?"

Matt sighed and pulled the little girl against his side. "No, princess. You're much prettier than that."

Shelby started to comment, then her gaze fell on Cassidy. The child really was beautiful. Her large, dark blue eyes were rimmed with long lashes, framed in a heart-shaped face. A sweet, happy smile reflected her bubbly personality.

Shelby thought about the photo she'd created on the screen. Matt was right. Cassidy bore no resemblance to the perfect image she'd created. Cassidy was real, blessed with an attractiveness no program could improve upon. She'd never thought about the difference between normal little girls and the airbrushed faces that appeared on *Tween Scene'*s covers. Suddenly turning sweet Cassidy into a too-perfect cover image seemed wrong.

"Cassie, honey, why don't you go on to your room. Miss Shelby and I will finish up in the kitchen."

"Cool. I want to tell Darcy about this picture."

The moment his child was out of earshot, Matt

pinned her with a stony glare. "What is this?" He waved the picture in air. "She looks like she's sixteen. I didn't recognize her."

Shelby's defenses kicked in. "I was showing her how we alter images for the covers of the magazine."

"And you thought it would be a good idea to make Cassidy look like some anorexic pop star?"

"No. It wasn't like that. She found out I was the editor of *Tween Scene* and she said she wanted to look like the girls on the covers. So, I took her picture and showed her how we augment the image for the best result."

"Augment? My little girl doesn't need to be augmented."

"Of course not. I only thought that if I—"

Matt held up his hand. "I don't expect you to understand, and I know you probably didn't think you were doing anything wrong, but my daughter is growing up fast enough. She doesn't need to be rushing things. One of the reasons I moved back here was to keep her from the destructive influences of the big city."

"It was a little harmless fun."

"Harmless? Really?" Matt exhaled slowly. "You've basically told her she's not good enough as she is. You've shown her that unless she looks like a movie star or a model, she's not acceptable. Is that really what you were trying to accomplish?"

"No, of course not." How could he even think such a thing? It was insulting. "I do this kind of thing all the time with our models."

"Shelby, Cassidy is a real little girl. Not a seasoned professional like you're used to dealing with. She's very vulnerable at this age. She has enough things assaulting her self-image. She doesn't need any more to confuse her."

Is that what she'd done? Had she confused Cassidy? In making her look perfect, had she done more harm than good? The truth in Matt's words filtered into her heart, filling her with regret. But Matt was overreacting.

"Matt, I'm sorry. I didn't mean any harm. But Cassidy is at an age when she wants to experiment with clothes and makeup and hairstyles. It's natural. I'll talk to her. Make sure she understands the difference between real life and magazine pictures." She'd come to care for her too much. The last thing she wanted was to be a bad influence on Matt's little girl.

Matt ran a hand through his hair and sat down on the arm of the sofa, clasping his fingers together tightly. "This is when I miss Katie the most. Cassidy needs a mother. I'm not sure I can provide her with everything she needs."

Shelby longed to reach out and touch him, give him comfort and reassurance, but she doubted he'd accept it. "But you'll marry again someday and—"

"No."

The steely determination in his dark blue eyes stunned her. He couldn't be serious. "But why? You're still young and there's so much life ahead for you."

The muscle in Matt's jaw flexed rapidly. "I'll never risk losing someone I love again. Watching her slowly waste away, knowing there was nothing I could do to help. I won't put my children through that a second time."

He turned away, but not before she saw the raw sorrow in his eyes. His pain scratched across her heart. "I'm sorry. But the chances of anything happening again…"

"Are too great."

Now she understood his protective attitude toward

his children. Matt stared at her a long moment, then stood, slipping his hands into his pockets. "I appreciate what you did today, helping Cassidy with supper and all. Just don't encourage her to look older and more sophisticated. She a little girl. I'd like to keep her that way as long as I can."

Her heart ached for him. He was guarding his family the only way he knew how. By being their protector. "All right."

Picking up her belongings she walked out, grateful that it was the weekend. She needed some distance from Matt and his kids.

Matt scooped up his son's dirty clothes from the bathroom floor and tossed them into the hamper. "Go get in bed. I'll be right in."

"Okay." Kenny dashed off to his room.

Matt headed down the hall, glancing into Cassidy's room. She'd decorated it herself, with his help. The walls were painted in pink, aqua and blue horizontal stripes. Gauzy fabric draped down from above the headboard. A pink fuzzy lamp and a purple futon finished the decor. It was garish and tacky and completely girly. Cassidy loved it.

He doubted Katie would have approved. She had favored elegant, traditional furnishings and decor. Matt had only wanted to make his little girl happy. Stepping inside the room, he smiled at the sight of his daughter stretched out on her bed, ankles crossed in the air as she watched her favorite television program. "As soon as this is over, lights out, young lady. Understood?"

She nodded absently. "Yes, sir."

He moved to the bed and touched the top of her head.

"That was a great meal tonight. I'm proud of you." Her dazzling smile melted his heart.

"Thanks, Daddy. I'm going to learn to cook more things so I can have your supper ready when you get home."

"That's sweet, but concentrate on being a kid first. Worry about my stomach later."

"Love you, Daddy."

"Love you."

Kenny was playing with Chester on the bed when Matt entered his room. His son's room was another matter. The boy was fascinated by reptiles and critters. He loved trees and the woods and would spend every moment there if he could. "What story are we going to read tonight?"

"The slingshot and the giant."

Matt smiled. He was pleased his son enjoyed the Bible stories. In the years after Katie's death they had drifted away from church attendance. It had been one of the things he was determined to change now that they were back home. He wanted his kids to grow up in the faith. He was ashamed that he'd allowed them all to backslide.

Matt finished the story then leaned down to kiss the boy's cheek. "Sleep well, sport."

"Daddy, can I watch *Insect Man* for a while? It's the weekend."

The cartoon superhero who could turn into any bug he wanted was his son's favorite. "I guess so."

Matt stood, signaling to Chester to follow. "See you in the morning." Matt shut the door and started down the stairs. The moment he entered the kitchen he stopped cold, bombarded by images from his unusual homecoming.

Walking into his home this evening had been surreal. The air had been heavy with delicious aromas, the atmosphere warm and welcoming. His children had scurried about the kitchen smiling and laughing. The scene had wrapped around his soul and filled him with such a longing he'd nearly buckled under the weight of it. For the first time since he'd moved back to Dover, this house felt like a home. He'd tried his best to make the place warm, cozy, a safe haven. But tonight it had been real.

And he had Shelby to thank for that. Cassidy and Shelby both had insisted the meal was his daughter's idea. He didn't doubt that, but Shelby had supervised and given all the credit to Cassidy. The pride and joy revealed in Shelby's face had captivated him. She had been genuinely delighted at his little girl's accomplishments. Matt poured a glass of tea, glancing out the window to the house next door.

He'd seen the friendship growing between his children and Shelby. He didn't want her to be friends with his kids. Yet her presence was firmly implanted in the space. Like she'd claimed it. He wasn't sure he liked that.

But he wasn't sure what to do about it.

Chapter Four

Shelby awoke the next morning well rested and feeling like her old self. She and Gramma had settled in on the sofa and talked. Gramma must have sensed her reluctance to discuss Matt and instead had caught her up on all the changes that had taken place in Dover since she'd left.

But memories of the family dinner at Matt's still played in the back of her mind. It had been a rollercoaster evening emotionally. First joy at Cassidy's success, regret over the enhanced picture and sadness as she listened to Matt speak of his wife and vow never to risk his heart and lose another woman he loved. She could only imagine how difficult that had been for him.

She pulled her hair up into a ponytail, then moved to the dresser and reached for her pills. The bottles were nearly empty. What would Matt do if he knew about her heart disease? If she didn't get control of her health, she was flirting with serious consequences, even death. Matt would probably forbid her to be around the kids at all. It would have become his worst nightmare—allowing his kids to bond with a woman who could die unexpectedly.

She loved being with Cassidy and Kenny. Being denied their company would break her heart and take a large measure of enjoyment out of her life. Better for everyone that she keep her health issues to herself.

Last night had helped her turn a corner. Her future still weighed heavily on her mind, but being home again, around Gramma and the kids, gave her renewed hope and a sense of belonging she'd been lacking. For all her busyness in New York, she'd always felt alone. Her work had consumed all her time, thought and energy, leaving her with few friends and no social life. Not even church. She hadn't realized until now how one-dimensional her existence had become.

But today was a new day. The weekend. She didn't have to worry about Matt or his children until Monday. Today she would focus on her health and start exercising. Shelby groaned. Of all the things she hated to do, exercising was at the top of the list. Right behind giving up regular coffee and sweets. She'd never been very athletic. The only time she'd enjoyed outdoor activities was when she and Matt—better not think about that.

Gathering her sagging determination, Shelby reviewed her plan. She'd start with a five-mile jog around Shiloh Lake outside of town. If she increased it a mile each day, by the end of the week she would be up to ten miles. That should get her back in shape quickly. Encouraged, she finished dressing, grabbing up her iPod and earbuds before hurrying downstairs.

Ellen was at the sink, and she raised her eyebrows as she scanned her from head to toe. "Well, what are you dressed for?"

Shelby poured a cup of coffee, doctored it with skim milk and a packet of artificial sweetener and took a sip. It was still awful. "I'm starting my exercise today."

Gramma nodded slowly. "Good. But don't overdo it. I know you. You'll want to start out with a ten-mile jog."

Shelby nearly choked on her coffee. When would she remember that Gramma could always read her like a book? "I was thinking more like five miles."

Ellen shook her head. "Honestly. I don't know what it is about this family that makes them think everything has to be done quickly. There is nothing wrong with taking life slow." She rinsed out her coffee mug and set it in the drainer. "Start with a leisurely stroll into town or walk the trails in the park. Each day you increase the distance and the pace until you're stronger. Then you can graduate to running like a track star."

Shelby smiled. "That takes too long."

Gramma crossed her arms over her chest. "This isn't a deadline you have to meet. This is your life."

Deadline. That's exactly how she'd been thinking of it. She'd given herself six weeks to learn to relax so she could get back to work. Probably not the best approach for someone in her condition. "Okay, how about a walk then. Slow and steady, like a turtle."

Gramma smiled. "Better. You could start with the trails out back. There's a shortcut at the tree line. But first, I've fixed you a healthy breakfast. Come and eat."

Shelby stepped onto the front porch, inhaling the heady scent of sweet olive that grew at the side of the house. The slight breeze also carried a hint of fall. Her favorite time of year, when the scorching heat of August was replaced with the balmier temps of September. She'd always been eager for school to start even though she hadn't fit in with most of the other kids. She'd felt at home in the classroom, studying and learning. Then at the end of each day, she'd hurry to Gramma's to sit in the sunroom or the porch swing and read magazines and eat cookies. It was a beautiful day, and she would try and think only beautiful thoughts. A walk was the perfect solution to her stress.

She started toward the back of the house, past the old garage, trying to remember what Gramma had told her about the shortcut to the trails that would save her the two-block walk to the main entrance. Friendship Park was a new addition to Dover. Once known as the Burton Farm, the city had purchased the land and turned it into a community park, complete with picnic areas, playground and hiking trails. She'd assured Shelby she couldn't miss the shortcut through the trees. She'd obviously forgotten her granddaughter's lack of experience with the outdoors.

"Miss Shelby. Where ya going?"

Shelby turned to see Kenny Durrant running toward her, Chester on his heels.

"I'm going for a walk."

"Are you going to the trails?"

She nodded. "My gramma said it was a good place to walk."

"It's cool. My daddy and I walk there lots of times. I could show you the way." Kenny beamed with excitement.

"That would be nice. But you'd better check with your father first." She glanced back at the garage behind Matt's house. A large SUV was parked in front of it today. Neither the rickety van nor the battered truck were anywhere to be seen.

"Okay, I'll be right back." Kenny darted off, his little legs pumping furiously. Shelby waited, even though she knew there was no way Matt would allow his son to go with her. Especially after the photo incident last night.

Kenny returned a few minutes later, his face flushed with excitement.

"What did your daddy say?"

"He said 'kay."

Shelby hesitated for a stunned second, glancing at the house, then back at Kenny. Maybe she'd misjudged Matt's attitude last night. Apparently he wasn't so angry that he would refuse to let Kenny go with her. That had to be a good sign. She shrugged. "Great. Let's get going then. Where's the shortcut?"

"I'll show you. It's way back there at the end of our yard." Chester took off ahead, apparently knowing the way.

Buoyed by the thought of having a companion on her first walk, she started off at a brisk pace.

"Hey! Hey!"

Shelby stopped and turned around. Kenny was several yards behind her, his short legs pumping to keep up.

"You walk too fast."

She hadn't realized she'd been moving so quickly. She'd have to watch that. She was used to doing everything at breakneck speed. Yet another life change she'd have to adjust to. "Sorry, Kenny. I'll slow down."

"Good, 'cause then I can show you the cool stuff."

He was an energetic child, alternately skipping and running, sometimes stopping abruptly. She found it difficult to walk in rhythm with the little boy's stride.

"We're here." Kenny stopped near the tree line, smiling broadly.

Shelby frowned at the wide opening between the trees and shrubs. It looked well traveled, but she didn't relish the idea of walking into the wilderness. "Are you sure?" She turned back to the twin houses positioned at the front of the large lots. They looked far off. Maybe this wasn't such a great idea after all.

Kenny waved her on. "Come on. It's right through here."

Shelby girded herself and followed. If a six-year-old could do it, so could she. Cautiously she stepped past the trees into the cool woods. She remembered these woods from when she was a child, but back then they'd been untamed and she'd braved them only once. Too many unknown sounds and movements had sent her racing back to the house.

"See," Kenny shouted, pointing. "There they are."

A few yards ahead stood a large wooden sign, the name of each trail and a corresponding map clearly engraved into the wood. Shelby quickly assessed the Camellia Trail as the longest. She started forward, but Kenny stopped her.

"This is my favorite one. You can trace the trail with your finger." He stepped to the sign and placed his index finger in the indented line on the map of the Magnolia Trail and traced the path. "First you go here, then you go up here, and then across here and down here, and then up here, and then down here again, and you're home." He smiled at her, pleased with himself.

His bright eyes and dazzling smile were infectious. She could see the resemblance to his mother in his coloring and green eyes and dimples. Cassidy favored Matt with her dark blue eyes and brown hair.

"Let's go. Come on, Chester."

They started down the Magnolia Trail. Kenny skipped ahead, Chester at his side. "Don't get too far ahead, Kenny." The gravity of being responsible for Matt's son suddenly struck her. She'd failed to consider the seriousness of taking the boy along. What had she been thinking? What if she lost him? What if something happened to him? How would she explain it to Matt? She quickly realized there was no need to worry. Kenny stopped every few steps to point out a special tree, to show her a log or to toss a rock into the shallow stream running parallel to the trail. At this rate it would take them all day to walk the half-mile trail. Kenny's preoccupation with nature would keep him close, but it was holding her back.

"Why do you run so fast?"

Shelby stopped and turned to find Kenny several yards behind her again. She hadn't realized she'd passed him. "I wasn't running. I was walking."

"Oh." Kenny frowned.

"We'd better get going. We've barely started our walk."

"Look, it's my favorite spot." He ran toward a bench at the edge of the creek. "Come on."

Kenny sat down. Shelby inhaled slowly, trying to quell her impatience. She sat, then glanced around. Trees. Water. Rocks. More trees. "This is nice, Kenny. Come on, we'd better go."

"No. You have to wait until the frogs come. Chester finds them and makes them ribbett."

Kenny sat patiently. Watching. Shelby tapped her toe. "Guess no frogs today." She stood. "We need to get to the end of the trail."

"Why?"

His question caught her off guard. "Because we're on a walk and we need to get to the end."

"That's no fun."

"Well, it's not about fun. It's about exercise. That's the whole point. I can think of a lot of things that are more fun than this. I'll bet you can, too."

Kenny shook his head, his expression serious. "No. Walking's not the fun part. The fun part is the looking."

She doubted that. She'd found nothing in these woods worth noting. It was merely a place to start walking, a means to work her way up to a longer, more strenuous level. Maybe she'd get a pedometer, then she could keep track of how much she increased her steps each day. Her little companion continued to stare at the creek. Perhaps a different tack would budge him. "We don't want to take too long or your dad will get worried."

Kenny hung his head and stopped swinging his feet. A sense of unease touched her nerves. He looked over his shoulder at her with a guilty expression. "I didn't tell Daddy."

"What!" This couldn't be happening. She put a hand across her mouth. The possible ramifications settled in her stomach like a stone. "Oh, Kenny. You told me he said it was okay."

"He was working and told me to wait a minute, but I was afraid you'd go without me."

"Kenny, you know that telling fibs is wrong."

"I know." Green eyes welled up with tears. "Is Jesus mad at me?"

"What?" Why did his every question throw her a curve? And how did she answer that one? "Uh, no. He's not mad. He's disappointed like I am and your dad will be, but none of us are mad." She thought back to a time when what Jesus thought of her mattered. "Jesus loves you."

Kenny came to her side and took her hand. "My mommy is with Jesus."

Shelby bit her lip against the stab of sadness in her heart. "I know, Kenny. Come on. We'd better hurry back." Thankfully, they hadn't traveled too far down the trail before Kenny had dropped his bombshell. They started back at a steady clip. Kenny kept pace, holding her hand the whole way.

She heard Matt calling for Kenny as they stepped through the trees at the property line. She could see him up near the house, jogging in different directions, searching for the boy. His body language told her how worried he was. Matt would be furious. How could she have let this happen? "Kenny, you run ahead and let your daddy see you're all right. I'll come and explain to him what happened."

Kenny nodded and ran ahead across the large lawn. "Here I am, Daddy."

Shelby hung back, walking slowly, watching as Matt jogged toward his son, grabbing him in a tight hug, his relief evident in the way he held him close to his chest for a long moment. His anger quickly became apparent when he set the boy down, his large hands gripping little shoulders, obviously demanding an explanation.

Shelby was glad for the vast yard between them. She didn't want to hear Kenny being scolded even if it was his fault. By the time she crossed the distance from the woods to the house, Kenny was apologizing.

"I'm sorry, Daddy."

"It's my fault, Matt. I thought—"

Matt took a menacing step toward her. "Did you think you could walk off with my son and not tell me?"

Shelby bristled. "That's not how it happened."

Matt planted his hands on his hips. "What were you thinking?"

"Daddy?"

Matt turned to his young son. "Go in the house. I'll be there in a minute."

"But Daddy…"

"Kenny. Do as I say."

Shelby's heart ached for the child. "Matt, don't blame him. He was—"

"I don't blame him. You should have known better. I guess I should be grateful you didn't run off and leave him in the woods alone. That's your usual response, isn't it? Change your mind and walk away?"

Shelby braced herself against his harsh words. He had every right to be angry at her for her actions fifteen years ago, but not where Kenny was concerned. "That's not fair. I would never leave Kenny alone. You have no right to even suggest such a thing."

Matt glared. "I have every right. He's my son."

Shelby tried to control her rising anger. She had to remember Matt was reacting out of fear and a lack of information. She couldn't imagine what he must have gone through when he discovered Kenny missing. "If you'll only calm down and let me explain, you might—"

"Since when do you bother to explain anything, Shelby? That's not your style." Matt set his jaw and turned away.

Shelby grabbed his arm and forced him around to face her. "And you're as bullheaded as ever. Do you want to hear what happened or not?"

"I know what happened."

Shelby pursed her lips together to keep from saying something hateful. "No. You don't. But when you decide you want to, you know where to find me." She turned on her heel and walked off. The chasm between them was as wide and as deep as ever.

The realization broke her heart.

Matt watched Shelby leave, regretting his harsh words. He hadn't meant to lash out at her that way, but something had come over him. Years of pent-up anger and resentment had erupted from deep inside, blindsiding him with their intensity.

He ran a hand down the back of his neck and turned back to the house. He'd been on the verge of panic, wondering where Kenny had gone. If anything happened to his children— He couldn't allow himself to think of those things. He'd never survive a loss like that.

It wasn't unusual for his son to wander to the edge of their acre lot and not hear when he was called. He was an imaginative boy, and sometimes he didn't pay attention, but he'd never gone to the trails by himself. He knew they were off-limits unless with an adult.

Kenny sat slumped in a chair at the table when Matt entered the kitchen. He looked so little. So vulnerable. His heart swelled with a love so intense it stole his breath. It helped temper his anger and fear at Kenny's disappearance.

He sat down across the table from the boy, clasping his hands together on the surface. "So, you want to explain to me why you broke the rules and went to the trails without asking?"

Kenny looked up, his green eyes, so like his mother's, filled with sadness. "I asked."

Matt frowned. "I don't remember you asking me."

Kenny nodded. "You were at the computer and I asked if I could go with Miss Shelby to the woods."

"I don't remember that, son."

"You were busy. You said to wait."

Memory surfaced. He'd been completely absorbed in bookkeeping for Handy Works when Kenny had dashed into his home office. He should have paid closer attention. "So why didn't you wait?"

Kenny shrugged. "She would have gone without me and I like the woods."

"I know you do, but you were wrong to go without permission. And Miss Shelby shouldn't have taken you with her without making sure I said it was okay."

Tears filled Kenny's eyes and trickled down his cheeks. "I told her you said I could go."

Shock and disappointment lanced through him. Kenny had never behaved like this before. The daddy in him wanted to pull the boy to his heart and hold him, chase away the tears. The parent in him understood that this was an opportunity to teach a lesson. "Kenny. You told her a lie, didn't you?"

He nodded, the tears flowing more now.

"We don't do that in this family. We follow the rules, and we tell the truth. I'm very disappointed. You won't be allowed to go the trails for a week. Is that clear?"

Kenny nodded, his lower lip quivering.

Matt's heart caved. "Come here, sport." He wrapped his arms around the slender boy and lifted him onto his lap. "I love you very much, but I want you to learn to do the right things."

Kenny sniffed and wiped his nose. "Miss Shelby was disappointed, too."

"What do you mean?"

"We were sitting on my favorite bench and I told her you didn't know I was with her. She got upset and we started back. She said you'd be disappointed, but that you'd still love me like Jesus does."

Matt winced with a sudden surge of shame. He shouldn't have jumped to conclusions. Kenny was the culprit in this adventure. Not Shelby. She had tried to explain, but he'd allowed his old hurts to override his common sense. He'd been rude and spiteful. She didn't deserve that.

"She was right. I do love you and I'm not mad. I get worried, Kenny. I don't want anything to happen to you."

"Like it happened to Mommy?"

Matt braced himself against the old pain. "Yes. I want to make sure you're safe every minute. When I can't find you, I get very scared. Do you understand?"

"I don't want you to be scared, Daddy."

"I know." He hugged him close, kissing the top of his head.

Matt watched his son leave the room, painfully aware that he had some serious damage control to handle. He needed to apologize to Shelby, but he wasn't looking forward to it. Ever since he'd seen her standing on Ellen's front porch, his mind had been flooded with memories and his emotions in conflict.

He'd planned a future with her, planned his life around her, and she'd suddenly decided he was too small-town and broken their engagement. She'd left him twisting in the wind and wondering why. Why had she changed her mind? What had he done? His sweet, funny Shelby had become enraged, and he hadn't known why.

Matt stared at his clasped hands on the tabletop. Shelby was here now. He could ask her outright why she'd turned her back on him, but what good would it do? They'd both gone on with their lives and found happiness. Knowing wouldn't change things.

Who was he trying to kid? Even after all these years it was the not knowing that still haunted him. As much as he hated to admit it, he wanted an answer. If he had an explanation, a reason for her behavior that night, then he could put it behind him once and for all.

It shouldn't matter. He'd gotten over her long ago. So why did his heart skip a beat whenever he thought about her? Why did his mind constantly replay sweet moments from their past?

Matt stood, scraping the chair legs across the floor. Because he was a fool with a bruised ego. He was also a man who needed to make an apology. And the sooner the better.

Shelby paced the kitchen, her emotions pulling her in two directions. One minute she was furious at Matt for refusing to listen to any explanation about Kenny. The next she wanted to cry over the lost hope of them ever being civil to one another. After today's incident with Kenny, he would never speak to her again, let alone allow her to help babysit. He was probably on the phone right now hiring a professional. Anxiety and frustration quickened her heart rate. She needed to move, to do something besides replay the ugly scene with Matt. How was she ever going to learn to relax with him next door?

Her gaze came to rest on her grandmother's small collection of pill bottles on the counter. Medications. She still needed to fill her own prescriptions. Now might be a good time to take care of that. A brisk walk into town might be exactly what she needed. She also needed to schedule an appointment with the cardiologist in Jackson her doctor had recommended.

Buoyed by her decision, she quickly changed into a denim skirt and a cool knit top and slid her feet into comfy sandals, grabbing her purse on the way out the door. By the time she reached the center of Dover she was feeling more relaxed than she had in a long time. So many landmarks along the way triggered sweet recollections from her childhood. Odd. She'd worked so hard to get away from this place. She'd been so firm in her resolve to stay away. Yet now that she was here, it felt like home. She felt like she belonged.

The picturesque downtown greeted her like an old friend. She strolled down Main Street past the furniture store and the bank, smiling as she glanced up at the name engraved in the stone lintel. It was the only building in town that spelled the name correctly. Do Over.

Originally a crossroad between the rail line to New Orleans and the wagon traffic from the river, the town had sprung up haphazardly overnight. When a fire destroyed most of the north side, the community saw it as an opportunity to begin fresh, a chance to do over their town more responsibly. The original name Junction City was replaced with Do Over, which was shortened to D'Over and eventually simply Dover. The irony didn't escape her notice. A do-over was exactly what she needed in her life right now.

Adam's Pharmacy was on the other side of the courthouse square, so she crossed the street and walked into the park. The historic gazebo nestled beside a giant magnolia beckoned her like an old friend. Shelby climbed the steps onto the bandstand, taking a slow turn around the perimeter. The gazebo was a landmark, one of the oldest structures in the town, and had become the symbol of Dover. It was as synonymous with Dover as the Dentzel Carousel was for Meridian and the lighthouse for Biloxi.

Everyone in town could trace many of their most important life events to the delicate structure. Her own catalogue was full of happy times with her parents when she was young, then with her friend Pam and lastly with Matt. Those memories didn't need to be visited right now. With an affectionate pat on one of the turned posts,

Shelby descended the wooden steps and started toward the drugstore again.

"Shelby. Shelby Russell!"

Turning to see who had called her name, Shelby smiled when she recognized her childhood friend. "Pam Cotter? I was just thinking about you."

The woman smiled happily and approached with arms spread wide. "I'd heard you were back. I couldn't wait to see you."

Shelby hugged her. "How did you know I was here?"

Pam pulled out of the embrace and grinned. "I work at the hospital. Your gramma practically announced it over the public address system."

Shelby nodded. "I should have known. How are you? I see you're still here."

"Yep. And it's Fleming now." Pam glanced at the bandstand. "How many Saturdays did we spend sitting in there eating ice cream and talking about how we would take the world by storm?"

"Too many to count. You look great. Married life agrees with you."

"Fifteen years and three kids." Pam surveyed her for a moment. "I've missed you, Shel. You left so suddenly. One day you were here, and the next you were gone. You didn't call or leave a note. Why? What happened?"

Shelby was beginning to see that she'd left another broken friendship in her wake. "I'm sorry, something came up and I left for college early." She smiled and changed the subject. "So you've been here in Dover the whole time?"

"Oh, no. Ron and I still went to State and got our degrees."

"I thought you gave that up when you got pregnant?" She remembered her bitter disappointment when Pam

had told her they wouldn't be roommates at college because she was pregnant and getting married instead.

"I did until the baby came, but Ron and I knew we
couldn't skip our education. He went on and I started a
year later, baby and all."

Her trip back to Dover was challenging many of the
reasons she'd left and making her wonder if there were
options she had never considered. Could she and Matt
have had it all? Each other, college and careers? Her
life could have turned out differently had she chosen
the other path. But she hadn't. She'd chosen college
and career and never regretted it a moment. "How did
you do it?"

"Believe me, I wouldn't recommend anyone get their
education the way we did. Living in married housing,
trying to raise a child and go to school and work. But
I'm proud of what we accomplished. What about you? I
hear you're some big magazine executive in New York."

"I am, but there's a big shake-up going on in the
company and I may be out of work soon." It felt good
to share that with her friend. They'd never had secrets
from one another.

"Oh, Shel, I'm so sorry. I know you were right there
at the top of your field." Pam squeezed her hand. "Are
you headed someplace special? I'd love to get a cup of
coffee and catch up."

It was on the tip of her tongue to decline, but the
opportunity to unburden herself was too appealing. "I
have to get some prescriptions filled. Why don't I drop
them off and meet you?"

"Great. The coffee shop is right there on the corner.
See you in a minute."

A short while later Shelby exhaled a sigh and looked
at her friend.

"So, everything in my life right now is in limbo." Shelby took a sip of her iced tea, enjoying the brisk taste and the sense of calm that washed over her. Pam had listened intently as she'd recounted the events that had forced her back home. "The worst part is feeling out of control."

"That's because you're still under the delusion that you have control at all. You don't have the power to change any of your problems right now, Shel, but He does. Let God work this out. But He can't do anything until you let go of it and let Him take over."

"You make it sound so easy."

"It's not easy, but it's necessary. Take things one step at a time. First off, concentrate on your health. Are you exercising?"

Shelby responded with a feeble shrug of her shoulders, which brought a knowing smile to her friend's face. "Here's my cell number. You can call me anytime. I walk every morning right past your grandmother's house. We can work out together. I'm here for you, Shel. Call me if you need anything."

"Thanks, Pam. I didn't realize how much I needed a friend." A shadow fell across the bistro table.

"Shelby Russell. Well, I'll be."

Shelby glance up into a pair of cobalt-blue eyes and a warm smile. "Mr. Durrant?"

Tom Durrant took her hand and squeezed it affectionately. "I didn't think I'd ever see you back in Dover again. What brings you to town?"

"I'm visiting my grandmother and taking a short sabbatical from work." It was the truth. Just not the whole truth. She swallowed her discomfort and smiled.

"It sure is good to see you." His eyes narrowed

slightly. "Are you doing all right? Everything okay with you?"

She smiled with as much reassurance as she could muster and introduced her friend. "I'm great. I see Mrs. Durrant's campaign signs all over town. Wish her luck for me." Mr. Durrant opened his mouth to say something but stopped. She suspected he had started to mention Matt and thought better of it.

"Will do. Oh, and if you're going to be around for the seventeenth we're having a shindig at Shiloh Lake to celebrate our anniversary. The whole town's invited. That includes you."

"Thank you." His sincere invitation cheered her. Mr. Durrant had always made her feel like one of his own. Shelby watched him go, her heart a tangle of conflicting emotions. She'd loved Matt's dad. One of her biggest regrets when she broke up with Matt was losing him as a father-in-law.

She looked over at Pam, who was studying her intently.

"So, did your sudden departure fifteen years ago have anything to do with Matt Durrant?"

Nodding slowly, she raised her glass to her lips. "Everything."

Chapter Five

Matt strode into the garage and stood at the workbench. He'd been promising Kenny he'd put up the tire swing for weeks now. But that wasn't why he'd decided to tackle it today. He needed to keep busy so he wouldn't think about the apology he had to make to Shelby. He pulled his tape measure out at the same moment his cell rang. He smiled at the name that appeared on the screen. "Hey, little brother. How's it going?" His brother was a police detective in Dallas. It was a high-stress job, but Tyler thrived on the challenge. "It's good to hear from you. What's going on?"

"The usual stuff. Chasing bad guys."

Matt heard something odd in his younger brother's deep voice. "Everything okay over there in Big D?"

"Yeah. I wanted to let you know I'm going to try and come home for Mom and Dad's anniversary shindig."

"Hey, that's great. They'll love that. It's been a while since you've been home."

"I know. I keep meaning to take a weekend off, but it never seems to work out. You know how it is."

"I do indeed. Hey, the kids will be glad to see you."

"I'm sure they've grown. Look, let's keep this a secret, okay? I'm not a hundred percent sure I can get the time off. I don't want Mom and Dad disappointed if I don't make it."

"No problem, but I'll be praying that it works out. I miss you, bro."

"Same here."

They said their goodbyes, and Matt sent up a quick prayer that Ty would make it to the picnic. Nothing would make his parents happier.

By the time Shelby returned to her grandmother's house later that afternoon, she'd regained her sense of contentment and had managed to keep thoughts of Matt and her career at bay for a few hours. She crossed the front porch and reached for the door handle.

"Shelby."

Matt. Her heart leaped into her throat. She should have known this moment of peace wouldn't last. This whole mess would have been so much easier if he wasn't next door. His boots scraped against the concrete as he mounted the porch steps. Heart pounding, she squared her shoulders and turned to face him. His cobalt eyes bored into her.

"We need to talk."

She shook her head. "No. We don't." She wasn't going to argue over this again. "I tried to explain to you what happened but you didn't want to listen. I'd forgotten how pigheaded you are."

"Shelby."

"Once you get an idea in that thick head of yours, there's no changing it. You charge ahead and won't listen to anyone. It's one of the reasons—" She crossed her arms over her chest and forged ahead. "I know you must have been frantic. I don't blame you, but how could you think for one moment that I would waltz off into the wilderness with your son without making sure he had permission? I know, I probably should have double-checked, but it never occurred to me that Kenny wasn't being truthful."

"Shelby."

"I did ask him, Matt. I really did but—"

"Shelby!"

"What?"

"Kenny told me what happened. All of it. I jumped to conclusions. I shouldn't have."

She blinked. "Oh." His apology was the last thing she'd expected.

"I reacted out of fear and concern for my son."

"I understand. Really."

He held her gaze a moment. "Good."

Shelby grasped the opportunity to bring up another matter she wanted to discuss. "Matt, maybe this is a good time to clear the air between us."

"Meaning?"

"Call a truce. Put the past behind us and move forward. Neither of us can change what happened." She tucked her hair behind her ear, searching for the right words. "I like your children. I like helping Gramma watch them after school, and I think they like me. Isn't that all that matters?"

He met her gaze and set his jaw. "Are you going back to New York?"

"I have a job there." Maybe.

"Right, and what's going to happen to Cassidy and Kenny when you suddenly pull up stakes and leave? They've already lost their mother. They don't need to grieve over someone else."

Shelby shook her head in disagreement. "Matt,

they're smart kids. They'll understand the difference between the death of a parent and a friend moving away." She faced him, holding his gaze. "The problems between us happened a long time ago. We shouldn't let our old resentments spill over onto the children. We're the adults here. Or at least we're supposed to be." Matt ran a hand through his hair and turned away. "Shouldn't we set aside the past and at least try and be friends? For their sake?"

Matt held her gaze a long moment before nodding. "All right. For their sake."

Shelby watched Matt walk away, bittersweet sadness encasing her heart. She'd hoped for a new beginning, a do-over of sorts, but she could see Matt was still unwilling to forgive her completely.

She sympathized with his desire to shield his children from emotional pain, but she wondered if his fierce need to protect was more about him than them. If only she could help him somehow. If only they could be friends again, talk things through the way they used to. Turning, she walked inside the house. There were no do-overs for them. She'd destroyed all hope for any relationship fifteen years ago when she'd given his ring back. She was beginning to think that was the biggest mistake of her life.

Matt picked up the cardboard box and carried it to the far corner of the Handy Works shed. He was helping his dad restock supplies. Setting the box on the workbench, he sliced it open and pulled back the flaps. Friends. She wanted to be friends. Not in a million years. But she was right about calling a truce. He couldn't keep flaring up like a porcupine whenever she was around, and he didn't want his kids caught up in their past.

He stared into the carton of nails. The tension between them still vibrated along his nerves. Something about her bothered him. More than the simple fact that whenever he was near her, his heart did strange things and his blood warmed as if standing next to a fire. He could dismiss that as simple attraction. A leftover reaction from when he'd been in love with her. It meant nothing. What puzzled him was his unshakable feeling that she needed protecting.

Shelby had always been focused and determined. She'd possessed a self-confidence far beyond her years. It was one of the things that had attracted him to her. She was completely different from the silly girls he'd dated in high school, and the coeds he'd met his first two years in college. But he'd sensed much of her bravado was a cover for her insecurities. That realization had always made him feel protective toward her. An assumption he'd learned the hard way was a lie. Shelby Russell didn't need anyone. She was perfectly capable of taking care of herself.

So what was triggering this desire to protect?

"Son, are you going to put those boxes of nails on the shelf, or are you just going to stare into the carton for a while?"

"Sorry, Dad. I've got a lot on my mind."

"Hmm. Shelby Russell?"

"How did you know?"

His dad leaned a hip against the counter and looked at him. "I saw her in town this afternoon. It was good to see her again."

"Yeah. Great." Apparently no one viewed her return the same way he did.

"Oh. I see. Well, I wanted to find out if you knew why she was back?"

"She says an overdue vacation. Why? What did she tell you?"

"She said she wanted to spend time with her grandmother." Tom shook his head. "But I don't know."

Finally! Someone else who shared his doubts. "You don't believe her?"

"How does she look to you?"

Beautiful. Delicate. Like a balmy spring day. Matt rubbed his forehead. Where had that come from? "I didn't really notice. We've only spoken a few times."

"She doesn't look well to me," Tom observed. "She's too pale, and that sparkle is missing from her eyes. Something's not right there. Your mom grew concerned when I told her, so I thought I'd check with you."

Matt set his jaw. "She's fine as far as I know."

"Your mom mentioned that she and Ellen are watching the kids for you in the afternoons. That's convenient."

"Yeah, but I'm still looking for alternatives."

"Oh. Why? I thought the kids liked Ellen."

"They do. It's Shelby I'm concerned about."

"Why's that?"

Matt pulled out a handful of boxes and shoved them to the back of the shelf. "Because my kids already like her, and knowing her, she's likely to run back to New York without any warning and leave them brokenhearted. I don't want them to lose someone else they've grown close to."

His father nodded, then turned and faced him. "So you think you need to protect them?"

"Yes. They've been through enough."

"Son, you know you can't protect people from caring about others. No one has that power."

"I can try."

Tom came and stood by Matt's side. "Are you sure this is about protecting their hearts or your own?"

The sanctuary of Hope Chapel wrapped around Shelby like one of Gramma's hugs the moment she stepped inside the old church off the square Sunday morning. Her grandfather had been the minister here for decades. It was as familiar as her grandmother's home.

She settled into the pew near the middle, sadness welling up in her heart. How had she strayed so far from her faith? When had she wandered off the path and ignored the beliefs she was raised with?

Gramma smiled over at her, and Shelby clasped her slender hand in hers, taking comfort from the contact. It hadn't been an intentional decision. Nothing had occurred to cause her to reject her faith. She'd simply drifted away until it wasn't even a part of her existence. Being here now made her realize what was lacking in her life—her connection to her Lord.

The organist began to play. Shelby recognized the hymn immediately. "Come Thou Fount of Many Blessings." It had been one of her favorites. One verse came sharply into her mind, the one about being prone to wander from God.

The words and the notes reverberated through her soul, reminding her of truths she'd too long ignored. She had wandered, and somewhere along the road she'd completely left God behind. Gramma had suggested that her current trials could be the Lord's way of pulling her back to Him. Maybe she was right after all.

Maybe what she needed was the strength and comfort only He could give.

Her gaze drifted toward the family sitting a few rows ahead. Matt and his children. Cassidy was whispering to the little girl beside her. Kenny had his head resting against his father's shoulder. The sight warmed her heart but left her with a strange sense of isolation. Shelby turned her attention to the elder as he stepped to the pulpit, only half listening as he reminded the congregation about the youth group outing and family-night supper.

"And now I believe Matt Durrant has an announcement."

Shelby jerked her head up as Matt walked briskly to the pulpit. He smiled. Her heart stopped. In his dark suit, crisp white shirt and patterned tie he looked professional, as comfortable in the boardroom as he'd looked in work clothes.

"Good morning. I want to remind you that we are always in need of volunteers for the Handy Works ministry. We still have a few slots open for the end of the month. Anyone who is handy with a hammer, a rake or a paintbrush, we can use your help. Call the church office or leave a message with our answering service. Thank you."

The lump of shame in Shelby's throat nearly choked her. She bowed her head, afraid to look at Matt. How he must despise her. She'd arrogantly assumed that he was nothing more than a handyman. No wonder he'd been so curt and gruff each time they'd spoken.

Forgive me, Father. Apparently the Lord was trying to get her attention on several levels. Maybe it was time she stopped resisting her situation and followed

Gramma's advice. Give it over to the Lord and trust in His wisdom. Do her part and let Him do his.

An hour later, Shelby came downstairs and went into the kitchen. "Anything I can do to help?" Gramma was still in her church clothes as she prepared Sunday dinner.

"Why don't you finish peeling these potatoes while I change?"

Shelby glanced into the pot. "That looks like a lot of potatoes for the two of us."

Ellen smiled and bobbed her eyebrows up and down. "That's because it's not. I want you to run next door and ask Matt and the children to come for dinner."

Shelby whirled to face her grandmother. "You want them to eat with us?"

"Certainly. I often have them over."

Shelby released a nervous sigh as her grandmother disappeared from the room. She and Matt had reached a truce of sorts and they had shared a meal the other night when Cassidy had cooked, but that seemed very different from having them at her gramma's dinner table. A meal here meant family, friends, closeness. At the very least it would have been better if Gramma had invited them herself.

Quickly, she finished preparing the potatoes, then braced herself to deliver the invitation. Well, she'd see just how solid their new truce actually was. Maybe Matt already had other plans. Maybe he'd refuse. Maybe he wasn't even home.

She'd seen him as they were leaving church that morning, but they hadn't spoken. Cassidy and Kenny had waved and smiled. Matt had nodded from across the sanctuary, his expression unreadable.

She knocked on the door, holding her breath. She

prayed Cassidy would answer. No such luck. Matt stood there before her, tall, handsome, causing her heart to ache for what could have been. She inhaled a whiff of his aftershave and lost her focus. "Uh. Hi. I, that is, Gramma wanted me to invite you to—you and the children—to dinner. But I'll understand if you have other plans. I know this is short notice, so don't feel obligated." Matt stared at her so long she began to squirm under his scrutiny. Thankfully, Chester scooted out the door and propped his paws on her knees. "Hey, fellow. How are you?" She glanced up at Matt to find his expression had softened somewhat.

"Sure. We'll be right over. The kids love having dinner with Ellen."

"Oh, well, good. It'll be ready in about half an hour."

He nodded. "We know the drill. I'll bring the salad."

"What?"

"That's our usual contribution to the meal."

"Oh. Okay then. Bye."

Shelby turned and went down the steps, not knowing how to feel about his acceptance. She'd been fully prepared for him to refuse simply because she was asking. It might be an uncomfortable meal. She'd just have to make the best of it. She was the outsider here. She'd cut herself off from this life, run away and never looked back.

No, that wasn't true. She'd looked back several times and wondered if she'd made the right decision. Doubts had plagued her so relentlessly that the only way she'd been able to deal with them was to block everything out. Dover and Matt simply didn't exist.

A half hour later they were all seated around the large dining room table saying grace. Shelby absently moved her food around on her plate as the conversation swirled around her. Cassidy and Kenny chatted about their friends and their school. Matt and Gramma discussed local issues and his mother's campaign. Shelby might as well have been invisible.

"Shelby Kay, you remember Clara Wilkins, don't you? She had the fabric store next to the card shop."

Shelby shook her head, uncomfortably aware of all eyes on her. "No, I don't remember her."

"Oh, I guess you were off at college about that time."

Shelby groaned inwardly. The one point in time she did not want to bring up with Matt at the table. The conversation continued, leaving her on the outside. Cassidy and Kenny took over the discussion, telling funny stories about Chester. Shelby braved a glance at Matt. He was watching his children with a pride in his eyes that hurt her heart. Every word they spoke, every gesture and smile, brought a light to his eyes. It was obvious to anyone who cared to look that Matt loved his children with his whole being.

She remembered a similar light in his eyes once when he looked at her. But she'd walked away from that love. Odd. She'd left Dover to find everything she'd ever dreamed of. Now she was wondering if what she really wanted had been here all along.

"It's a wonderful ministry, Shelby."

Shelby pulled her attention back to her grandmother. "Ma'am?"

"Handy Works. Matt and his family started it a year or so ago, and it's been such a blessing to this town."

Shelby glanced at Matt. He was staring at her, and she thought she saw a smirk on his face.

"We have a number of elderly and poor in our community who can't afford to hire people to do yard work or repairs on their homes," Matt explained. "We provide that for them. Thankfully we're also blessed with a large number of people who are willing to share their time and skills to help out."

Shelby swallowed her pride. "It's a wonderful thing you're doing."

"Thanks, but it's only a small ambition."

Heat infused her cheeks. Would he never let her forget those cruel words? Gathering her courage, Shelby decided to assert herself. "So what *do* you do for a living, Matt?"

"Daddy's a teacher," Kenny chimed in. "He teaches at a grown-ups' school."

Matt pinned her in place with his navy blue gaze.

"I teach at the local community college during the week and a few online classes at night." One corner of his mouth twitched as he stared at her. "I have a full slate of classes this semester, but normally it's part-time. I want to spend as much time with my kids as I can. They're my only ambition now."

There it was again. That dig at her harsh words from long ago. Shelby decided that silence might be the best course of action for the rest of the meal. She'd been stung enough for one day.

Matt glanced across the table at Shelby, regretting his sarcastic comment. Her gaze was focused on her plate, but he could see the dejected slump to her shoulders. She'd been silent most of the meal, only speaking when spoken to and then responding in clipped tones. She had made few attempts to enter into the conversation.

Their small-town topics obviously bored her. She was too worldly for the likes of Dover. Matt took a sip of his tea, remembering the stunned look on her face when he'd been addressing the congregation about

Handy Works. He'd taken a smug satisfaction at the time from putting her in her place. He was ashamed of that now. It was out of character for him to play those games. They'd agreed to a truce, to behaving like adults, and he wasn't holding up his end of the bargain.

"Dad, can Miss Shelby come to Gramma and Grandpa's special picnic?"

Matt stared at his plate a long moment. How was it that children could always ask the wrong questions at the wrong time? "I'm not sure if Miss Shelby will still be here for the picnic, Cassidy. She has an important job she has to go back to." Shelby shot him a glance filled with fire, her expression dark and challenging.

"I have no immediate plans to leave."

Matt stifled a grin. His gibe had hit a nerve. "Aren't you anxious to get back to the big city?" He still wasn't convinced that she would hang around for the six weeks she had mentioned. He was prepared to wake up one day and find her gone. No explanation, no goodbye.

Shelby raised her chin. "Actually, I'm finding my time here very relaxing."

"That's news to me," Gramma muttered with a frown.

"Well, can she?" Cassidy asked again.

"Can she what?" Matt had forgotten the question.

"Can she come to Gramma and Grandpa's party?"

Matt watched as defiance bloomed in Shelby's eyes and smiled inwardly. She'd want to come to the picnic now simply because he didn't want her to. That was the Shelby he remembered.

Kenny spoke up. "Daddy, can Chester come to Gramma and Grandpa's picnic? He likes to chase the ducks."

Matt stabbed at his food. "I don't know. We'll see."

"Is this the anniversary picnic?" Shelby looked at Matt and smiled. "I saw your dad yesterday. He invited me."

Touché. She'd outmaneuvered him. To refuse an invitation now would be rude. "You're welcome to come. The seventeenth, right after church. Shiloh Lake."

Shelby smiled. "I'll be there." She stood and carried her plate from the room.

Matt followed, stopping beside her at the kitchen sink. "You want to tell me what that was all about?" She didn't look at him.

"I love your parents. I wouldn't miss a celebration in their honor."

"That's not what I meant and you know it."

She turned and smiled. "Oh?"

Matt crossed his arms over his chest. "Suddenly you find our small town relaxing and you might stay on? Ellen seemed surprised by that."

"I don't have a specific date to go back." She shrugged, reaching across him for another plate. "And I am starting to relax. I ran into an old friend yesterday, and I'm looking forward to spending time with her."

He caught a whiff of her perfume and stepped away. "Why are you really here, Shelby?"

She tossed the dishrag into the sink. "I told you. I'm here to rest and visit my grandmother."

"No." Matt shook his head. "There's something more to it."

Ellen breezed into the kitchen clicking her tongue. "I'll handle those dishes. Go outside and enjoy this beautiful day."

Matt turned and placed a kiss on Ellen's cheek. "It was delicious as usual. Thank you."

"I love having you. I also love cleaning up my own kitchen. Now scoot."

"We need to be leaving anyway. My mom is having a birthday party for my uncle Hank this afternoon and we still have to pick up a present."

Ellen glanced over her shoulder. "Tell the judge happy birthday for me."

"Will do. I'll see you tomorrow, Ellen, when I pick up the kids."

Shelby rested her head against the chain supporting the front-porch swing. The gentle swaying motion soothed her troubled thoughts. Once again she was forced to adjust her assumptions about Matt. He wasn't a handyman; he taught college students. The battered van wasn't his job; it was his ministry. What gnawed at her most was his pointed question on why she was really here. Maybe she should tell him she was on medical leave and be done with it. But what if he refused to let her watch the kids? What if he wouldn't even talk to her anymore? The thought saddened her. For all her intent to avoid him, now that they had reunited she didn't want it to end again.

The front door creaked as Ellen stepped out onto the front porch. "Well, it's good to see you relaxing without all those electronic gadgets in your hands." She eased down into the wicker rocker facing the swing. "What are you going to do the rest of the afternoon?"

"I don't know. I'm feeling lost. I don't know what to do with myself. For the first time in fifteen years, I have no direction. I have nothing to keep me busy."

"Well." Gramma chuckled softly. "If it's keeping busy that you want, there's plenty to do around here. I have a garden out back you could work in. Or you could volunteer to help with Matt's ministry."

Shelby smiled and shook her head. "I'm not handy with tools."

Gramma raised her eyebrows. "Your hand fits a rake, doesn't it? Not all the work they do is repairs." She stood and started back inside. "You can come help me with my scrapbook. All the things you need are right there on my desk in the corner of the living room."

"Thanks, Gramma, but I'll find something to do." Her gaze traveled to Matt's house. She'd better find it fast. She would not spend all her spare time thinking about Matt Durrant.

Chapter Six

Strange how one phone call could change so many people's lives. Gramma had only been gone an hour, but already the house felt sad and empty. Gramma's sister, Aunt Naomi, had fallen and broken her hip and her family had asked Gramma to come and stay with her during her recovery. After a hectic couple hours of packing and rearranging Ellen's various responsibilities, she'd left for Baton Rouge.

Gramma's absence not only left Shelby in charge of babysitting Cassidy and Kenny; it had opened up a new issue. Her health. She had to tell Matt the truth. She couldn't keep this from him now. He was already worried about his kids being hurt by her leaving. If something happened to her while she was watching the children, she'd put them at risk. She wasn't looking forward to breaking all this bad news to Matt when he got home. Once he knew about her heart problems, he would probably end her relationship with his kids. She hated to face that, but better now than when she'd totally lost her heart to them. She couldn't really fault him for wanting to spare his kids further trauma. But her own heart would be wounded in the process.

The afternoon loomed ahead, long and empty. She'd considered texting Matt about the change in babysitting arrangements, but she decided this kind of news was best done in person. The children would be home in a couple hours, so she'd take care of them and explain it to Matt when he got home. In the meantime, she had to do something to keep busy. The thought of telling Matt about Gramma leaving and her heart condition was making her anxious.

Shelby wandered through the hall into the living room. There was no sense trying to work; things at *Tween Scene* were still in limbo. She'd already gone walking with Pam early this morning and discovered that having a friend to talk to made exercising more enjoyable than she'd ever imagined. But what did she do now?

Her gaze fell on the table in the far corner. As she drew closer she saw that it was Gramma's scrapbooking project. The large book was filled with family photos, each page decorated with colorful papers and tiny ornaments. Beside the book was a clear plastic box. Shelby opened the lid to examine the contents. It was filled with all the things she would need. Paper, scissors and tiny decorations. The creative pages reminded her of the yearbook and the amateur magazines she'd made in school. She'd been skeptical when Gramma had suggested working on the scrapbook, but it might be fun. It might help her remember why she wanted to be involved with magazines in the first place.

The afternoon went surprisingly fast. It wasn't until the clock struck the hour that Shelby realized it was time for Cassidy and Kenny to get home from school. Dabbing a bead of glue on a small ribbon, she carefully laid it on the corner of a photo as the bus pulled up at the end of the drive.

* * *

Shelby's anxiety about talking to Matt disappeared in the enjoyment of being with the children. They'd had plans to walk the trails today, but a sudden rain shower had squashed that idea. Cassidy had suggested baking cupcakes and Kenny had embraced the idea, digging out all the sprinkles, colored sugar and anything else he could find to put on top of them. The result was a messy kitchen and breakfast table crammed full of goodies. Cassidy was pulling a freshly baked pan of cupcakes from the oven when Matt walked in the door.

"Hey, Dad. We're making cupcakes for dessert."

Matt set his briefcase and other items on the desk, glancing around the room. He was smiling, and Shelby took that as a good sign.

"So are cupcakes the main course tonight?" He glanced over at her.

"No. We pulled out one of the casseroles Laura left. I hope that's okay."

"Fine. How did it go today?"

"Good. I really enjoy watching them, Matt. They make it fun and easy." No sense postponing the news. "But we need to talk." She moved to the far end of the kitchen.

A deep troubled frown appeared on Matt's forehead as he joined her. "Something wrong with the kids?"

She quickly reassured him. "No. nothing like that. It's Ellen. She had to leave town suddenly. My great-aunt broke her hip and Gramma went to Baton Rouge to take care of her."

"I'm sorry to hear that. How long will she be gone?"

"A couple weeks, I'm afraid. Which brings me to the babysitting situation." It was clear from the expression on his face that it had sunk in. She would be the sitter from here on out.

He slipped his hands into his pockets. "I see. So what do we do?"

"Matt, I like being here for the children after school. We get along well together, and I'm perfectly willing to continue watching them. If you're all right with it."

Matt looked over at his children, who were busy decorating the cupcakes. Giggles and teasing conversation filled the air. She watched as his troubled expression slowly changed into affection. "Okay. But I have to be able to depend on you being here every day."

She tried not to be offended by his words. She understood how deeply he loved his children and how much he worried. "You can. But there's one more thing I need to make you aware of. Can we step outside?"

Matt frowned. "Okay. Let's go out to the front porch." He turned and faced her as soon as the door closed. "What's this about?"

"You've asked me why I came back to Dover. I came to stay with my grandmother because I'm on medical leave." She saw Matt tense, his eyes darkening. "I had a very mild heart attack caused by stress. Nothing serious, but it was a wake-up call. I was ordered to change my lifestyle and rest or the next time could be serious."

Matt's jaw flexed rapidly. "So you're saying you could have a fatal heart attack at any time?"

"No. There's nothing wrong with my heart. But I do have to make changes, take better care of myself. I have a family history of heart disease. I wasn't going to tell you since Gramma was doing the babysitting, but knowing how you feel, and what your children have been through, I thought I should tell you."

The muscle in his jaw flexed rapidly again. "I don't know what to say. This changes everything."

"It doesn't have to. My condition is treatable and stable. I'm on medications, and I'm following the doctor's orders."

"And what happens if you have a heart attack while you're with my kids?"

Shelby clasped her hands together, trying to stay calm. "The likelihood is remote. But that's why I told you. I'll be happy to keep watching the kids until you can find someone else. But I'm perfectly capable of caring for them. And I want to. I really like them, Matt. I wouldn't let anything happen to them."

"What if you can't help it?" Matt paced off, running a hand through his hair. "No. This won't work. I'll find someone else."

Her worst fear had come true. "I'm sorry. But I couldn't continue babysitting and not let you know." She moved to the door. "Let me know how you want to handle this. I'll be here tomorrow unless you've made other arrangements."

Matt crossed his arms over his chest and nodded. The grim set to his jaw told her he was struggling with the news. There was nothing left to say. After a quick goodbye to the kids, Shelby went home, relieved that there'd been no confrontation, no angry words. But her news had shifted their relationship and she could only pray that Matt would let her continue to watch Cassidy and Kenny until he found someone else. She hadn't realized how much a part of her life they'd become until now.

Matt went through the evening routine in a daze. Shelby was sick. A woman standing at the edge of death. This couldn't be happening again. He'd been concerned about Shelby walking out on his kids, now he had to worry about her dying. His mind flooded with memories of helplessness, pain and wrenching loss. He wouldn't survive it a second time. As soon as the kids were settled he would call his dad. He needed advice.

It was nearly two hours later before Matt had a chance to call his dad. He paced the kitchen, waiting for him to answer.

"Hey, son. What's going on?"

Matt took a deep breath. He was sure his dad would agree with him that he could not let Shelby watch his kids. "Remember when you said you thought Shelby looked tired? Well, turns out she's not back in Dover just to visit Ellen. She's on medical leave. She's had a heart attack and was sent here to rest up."

"What? But she's so young."

Matt paced the room. "She said it was brought on by stress."

"Well, that would make sense given her line of work. So how serious is this? Has she had surgery or anything like that?"

"No. Nothing like that. She said it was a very mild one and she was told to rest and change her lifestyle. But, Dad, she's watching my children every day. She's alone here with them. What if something happens?"

"Then your mom and I are right here to step in. But I think you might be worrying for nothing. From what you're telling me, her condition doesn't sound serious."

How could his dad say that? "She's had a heart attack. That sounds serious to me."

"Don't anticipate trouble before it happens. There are all levels of heart disease, and most are manageable. But if you're so concerned, you could get someone else to watch them."

"That's the problem. There isn't anyone at the moment."

"Then why not let things go on for the time being? I know your mom is busy with her campaign and I'm at the store all day, but we're still only a few blocks away. Tell Shelby to call us if she has any problems. Have a little faith, son. Relax and take it one day at a time."

Matt hung up the phone, his thoughts swirling like a hurricane. His father had always given him sound advice, but he wasn't sure he could follow it this time. How did he take things one day at a time when each day held the potential for disaster?

By Thursday afternoon, Shelby had renewed hope that things between her and Matt were going to work out. He'd questioned her about her condition, wanting assurances that she wasn't going to suffer another attack unexpectedly. She promised him she would call one of his parents the moment she experienced any symptoms. He had finally agreed to let the situation stand. In the meantime, he would continue to look for another babysitter.

It was more than she'd hoped for. Apparently he'd come to terms with things because he'd come home in a good mood the last few nights. He'd even asked her to stay for supper again. He'd fired up the grill and the grilled chicken had been too good to resist.

Today the children had opted to stay with her at Gramma's house. After releasing Chester from his cage, they'd gathered on the porch to discuss the day.

"I painted pictures at school and the teacher put them up on the wall."

"That's wonderful, Kenny. What did you draw?"

He stooped down and hugged his furry dog. "Chester. He's my best friend."

"What about you, Cass? Anything exciting at school today?"

The girl shrugged. "Molly got some new nail polish. It was yellow. Way cool. My teacher Miss Jenkins is getting married and she said we could all come to the wedding."

"How nice of her. When is the wedding?"

"Not till next summer. But we had to do collages about things we like, so some of us added wedding dresses to them. Did you ever do a collage?"

"I did. In fact, putting a magazine together is a lot like that. I'm working on my gramma's scrapbook and it's not too different. I'd love to see what you've done. Did you bring it home?"

"No. It's for the open house tonight."

"What open house? At school?"

"Yes. I brought the paper home for Dad to look at."

"Are you sure he saw it? Because I don't recall him saying anything about an open house. What time does it start?"

"Six-thirty. But it goes for an hour or so."

"Honey, he doesn't even get home until that time."

Cassidy grew edgy. "I know I told him. Everybody's parents are going to be there. It's like a huge deal." She scooted off the swing and darted inside, returning a few moments later with a wrinkled paper in her hand and a worried expression on her face. "I forgot to give this to him. Now he won't be there and I won't have a parent to show up." Tears welled up in her blue eyes.

Shelby motioned for her to sit beside her, taking the paper and scanning the information. Unless he could get off work early, there was no way he could get home and to the school in time. "Kenny, do you have an open house tonight, too?"

He nodded. "Did you tell your daddy?"

He shrugged. "I don't know."

Cassidy was weeping now. "I wanted him to see my collage and talk to my teacher. I'll be the only one there without a parent."

"Now, don't worry. We'll get it all sorted out. I'll text your father, and we'll see what we can work out." A few minutes later her cell rang and she took the call, walking to the far end of the porch so she could talk privately. "Matt? I'm sorry to bother you, but I just found out about this a few minutes ago."

"Why didn't she tell me sooner?"

Frustration was evident in his tone. "Is there any way you can leave early?"

"No. Not today. In fact I might be a few minutes late. I have a meeting with a student after classes."

There was an obvious solution, but Shelby was reluctant to suggest it. One glance at Cassidy's sad face made up her mind. "Matt, why don't I take the children to the school and you can come directly there as soon as you can? That way they'll feel better knowing you're on your way and I can stand in as the—" She didn't want to use the word *parent*. "The adult representative in the meantime."

The long silence on the other end of the phone spiked her anxiety. "All right. But are you sure you want to do this? It's a big imposition."

"No it's not. I'm curious to see the things the kids talk about every day. It'll be fun. As soon as you get there I'll leave. I don't want to see them disappointed."

"Neither do I. Okay, I'll get there as soon as I can.

And, Shelby, thanks. This'll mean a lot to the kids. And I appreciate it, too."

Cassidy and Kenny warmed to the idea and quickly helped get ready. After a quick meal and a change of clothes, they arrived at school with plenty of time. Shelby followed Kenny to his room first, admiring his artwork. She'd have recognized Chester anywhere. The little boy had captured him perfectly, scruffy tail and all.

She met his teacher and explained that his father was coming later and he'd probably want to speak with her. Cassidy was fairly jumping out of her skin to get to her room. Once there she darted off, then came back with two girls in tow.

"Miss Shelby, this is Molly and this is Darcy, my two BFFs." She turned and pointed to Shelby. "And this is my babysitter, Miss Shelby. She's the editor of *Tween Scene* magazine."

Squeals of appreciation and excited comments swirled around her. "I'm glad you enjoy the magazine, girls." She allowed the conversation to continue a few moments, then touched Cassidy's arm gently. "I want to see your collage, and then I'd like to meet your teacher. I want to tell her that your father will be here shortly."

Cassidy's collage was impressive. Shelby found herself swelling with pride at the young girl's ability. She was beginning to understand better Matt's fierce protective instincts. With a heart this full of love, how could you not strive to make your children's life the best they could be? She glanced around the room at the parents, noticing the pride and joy in their expressions as they examined the accomplishments on display. Even Kenny was smiling at the things he saw.

She'd always felt tremendous pride in her work and

in the magazine she produced. But none of her achieve-
ments had made her feel one-tenth as satisfied as seeing
what these two children had done. It was something she
was going to have to think about going forward. There
might be something more important than *Tween Scene*
and her career.

Matt took the steps to the second floor of Dover El-
ementary School two at a time. He only had a half hour
to visit both his children's rooms, admire their projects
and meet their teachers. He'd have a nice long talk with
Cassidy later about making sure notices from school
were given to him.

He stepped inside room 208, his gaze searching for
his daughter. He found her standing beside Shelby, talking with a young woman he recognized as Cassidy's
teacher, Miss Jenkins. He started forward, noticing how
his daughter leaned close to Shelby, glancing up at her
with a smile. Shelby smiled back, laying an arm across
the girl's shoulders affectionately. His heart tightened
in his chest. For the first time since Shelby had started
watching his kids, he realized that she genuinely liked
them and truly had their best interests at heart.

He also realized what his children were missing
without a woman in the home. The sight of his daughter and Shelby brought a warmth into his heart. Kenny
sidled up to Shelby and smiled up at her. She ruffled
his hair and pulled him close.

Mesmerized, Matt move forward, catching the tail
end of the conversation.

"I'm so glad to meet you, Mrs. Durrant."

"Oh no, I'm Shelby Russell. I watch the children after
school. I'm their neighbor. Mr. Durrant—"

"Is sorry to be late."

"Daddy!" Kenny raced toward him, hugging his waist.

Matt spoke with the teacher, then followed Cassidy to her display. Kenny was impatient to get back down to his room. There was barely time to view his pictures before the event was concluded.

Outside in the parking lot, they walked Shelby to her car and said goodbye with hugs and fervent thank-yous.

Matt pointed to his SUV, which was only a few cars down the row. "Go get buckled in. I'll be right there." He turned to Shelby, searching for the right words. "I can't thank you enough for stepping in at the last moment."

"I was glad I could fill in until you got here. It was important to them that you attend."

"But I couldn't have if I'd had to come home and get them first. I appreciate what you did. I'd forgotten how nice it was to know someone has your back. To pick up the slack. It's hard to be everything to them all the time."

"You're doing a great job, Matt. Don't ever question that."

He looked into her beautiful brown eyes and felt something deep inside shift. She'd always had his back, except once. "Thanks again. I'd better go. I'll see you tomorrow evening." Matt strolled over to his car. Shelby was good with his children, and they were happy under her care. But was it wise to let them care for someone who was battling a heart condition?

"Piz-za! Piz-za!" Cassidy and Kenny chanted loudly.

"Please can we have pizza for supper?" Cassidy begged. "I want to go to Angelo's."

Shelby laughed and held up a hand to silence the girl.

"I think it's a great idea, but we need to wait for your father to get home and see what he has to say." After the open house, she'd grown even closer to the children. Matt had been more pleasant, too, inviting her to share the evening meal each day. She'd gladly accepted, but she knew she had to back off some. It wasn't a good idea to become too entangled with their lives.

"Daddy will say yes," Kenny announced confidently. "He loves pizza."

"All right. But in the meantime, homework for you, missy. Kenny, you have some chores, remember?"

Shelby watched them scurry off, her heart filled with affection. She grew to love them more each day. But always in the back of her mind lay the knowledge that sooner or later she'd have to leave them, and Dover, behind. She would miss them and she believed they would miss her, too. A shroud of deep sadness settled heavily upon her spirit. "Lord, why have you put me here? Nothing good can come of this. A lot of hearts will be broken. Including mine."

Shelby went to the small table in the corner of Matt's living room, where she'd set up her scrapbooking supplies. The children were more comfortable in their own home, so she'd started bringing her scrapbooking supplies with her to work on in the afternoons. It helped to keep her mind off the fact that she was spending so much time in Matt's home. It was hard to maintain emotional distance when she was surrounded by his presence at every point. After all, she had to protect her heart, too. She was living a fantasy, seeing how her life might have gone had she made different choices. She'd come to realize the most exhilarating moment of her career was nothing compared to the joy and satisfaction she experienced with these children.

Cassidy appeared beside the table, a smile on her sweet face. But they weren't her children. Never would be. "Hi, sweetie. Homework all done?"

"Almost." She sat down in the chair and rested her elbows on the table. "Is that Miss Ellen's scrapbook?"

"It is." Shelby pivoted the large book so she could see the page better. Cassidy had never shown any interest in the book before. "I'm about finished with this page. This is my aunt and uncle, and that's my mother there."

Cassidy leaned closer for a better look. "Cool. Why did you put a seashell on the page?"

Shelby smiled at the memory. Her last happy one before her father left. "My whole family went to the beach that summer. We stayed in this big hotel for a week and swam every day. In the evenings we'd go out to eat, then play miniature golf or go to the amusement park."

"Could I do a scrapbook?"

What had prompted this sudden interest? "Sure. It's easy."

"Could we do one about my mom?"

Shelby froze, her heart contracting into a tight ball. "I think that would be a great idea. Kenny could help, too."

Cassidy nodded. "My dad's birthday is coming up. We could give it to him then."

Shelby smiled and gave the girl a hug. Cassidy had such a sweet, loving heart. "As soon as you finish your homework, we'll run into town and pick up a book." Cassidy's thoughtfulness brought tears to her eyes. Matt's children were so delightful. What a joy it would be to watch them grow up.

Cassidy pulled the last piece of clear plastic from the new scrapbook as Kenny charged into the room. Shelby had taken the children into town and selected a large scrapbook for them to work on. Each child had picked up a few trinkets and colorful paper to decorate the pages. Cassidy had chosen a sheet filled with hydrangeas because she said it was her mother's favorite flower. Kenny found a piece with books on it because he remembered how his mother would read to him. Shelby had been deeply moved by their sweet memories.

"Daddy's home." Kenny spun on his heel and headed toward the front door.

"He'll see our surprise." Cassidy's eyes filled with worry.

Shelby motioned her away. "You go. I'll hide this with my stuff and take it with me for the weekend. I'll bring it back on Monday." Quickly she gathered up her scrapbooking paraphernalia, meeting Matt in the foyer as he entered. Kenny hugged his daddy's hand. "Can we go get pizza?"

"I guess." Matt smiled, resting a hand on his son's head. "Go get ready."

She looked at Matt. "They've been begging for it all day."

"How did it go?" he asked as the kids drifted off.

"Good. Cassidy's homework is done. Kenny brought home an invitation to Andrew's birthday party tomorrow. I think it might have been in his backpack for a few days. I'll have to do a better job of looking in there."

"I'm not sure that would be safe."

She chuckled and nodded. "Other than that, I think all is well." She shrugged and shifted her cumbersome books and the small plastic box with photos and decorations.

"Can I help you with that?"

She shook her head. "It's not heavy. So, I'll see you

on Monday. Unless you've found someone else?" He stared at her a moment, making her feel uneasy.

"No. Not yet." He slipped his hands into his pockets. "Thanks for all you did this week. It means a lot to me that I don't have to worry about the kids while I'm at work. I know they're in good hands."

"I'm glad. I'm enjoying their company. I really care about them, Matt."

"I know you do. I can see that."

"Daddy, we're ready," Cassidy called, hurrying into the room, Kenny on her heels.

"Okay, okay." He smiled and held his hands up in defeat. "Give me a chance to change my clothes." He turned to her. "Thanks, Shelby."

"You're welcome."

Matt opened the door for her, but before she could move, Kenny spoke up. "I want Miss Shelby to come for pizza with us."

Cassidy nodded. "She has to come, Dad." She clasped her hands together dramatically. "Can she, Dad, huh? Please? She doesn't have anything to eat at her house."

Shelby cringed. That would teach her to confide too much in the children. "Oh, no, there's plenty of food. Just nothing I like." A hot flush filled her cheeks. Great. If that wasn't a weak refusal. He'd think she was angling to accept.

Matt met her gaze, a small smile on his lips. "I think that's a good idea. She's worked hard this week and saved the day at the open house. She deserves some Angelo's World Famous Pizza."

Shelby didn't know how to respond. Did he really want her to join them? He had been more pleasant the past few days. He'd even started calling in the afternoons to check on things, listening intently as she told him about the cute and funny things the children would do and say.

The tension between them had eased considerably. Some of their old friendship was starting to return. A result of the truce, no doubt. He'd agreed to the truce for the sake of the children. He would do anything for them, even be nice to her. But inviting her out in public, to a restaurant, was something entirely different. She looked down at the children's hopeful expressions. She would do it for their sake.

"Uh. Sure. I'd like that. I'll be right back."

Cassidy and Kenny cheered and jumped up and down. Matt glanced at his watch. "We'll leave in ten minutes."

She nodded, still questioning the wisdom of spending an evening with Matt and his children in what amounted to a family outing. She was playing with fire. How could she maintain her safe distance if they started behaving like a real family?

Chapter Seven

Matt quickly changed into jeans and a polo shirt, wondering what demented impulse had prompted him to include Shelby in the pizza trip. The last thing he wanted was to draw her even deeper into his family circle. He had a feeling it was already too late. He felt her presence in his home and in the lives of his children every night, long after she'd crossed the driveway and gone home. He just wasn't sure how he felt about that yet.

Outside on the front porch, Matt locked the door, then glanced up to find the object of his thoughts coming across the driveway. His heart stopped. She was so lovely. Her hair was down from its usual ponytail, swaying against the side of her neck with each step. Her eyes were bright with affection as she smiled at his son and daughter.

Cassidy bounded from the porch and greeted Shelby with a hug. "I'm so glad you're coming, too."

Shelby glanced over at him, and he returned her smile. He was probably worrying about nothing. She was doing a great job with the kids. She was dependable and caring. He'd stopped worrying that she'd disappear. And she'd reassured him repeatedly that she was doing all she could to take care of herself. And he liked the idea of having someone along this evening to talk to. An adult to converse with. A nice change from the chatter of his son and daughter.

Kenny grabbed her hand, claiming her attention. "I like the dessert pizza best."

As they started toward the car, Cassidy proposed a different plan.

"Dad, can we walk to town?"

His daughter's simple request caught him off guard. He looked at Shelby. It was a nice evening. Warm with a slight breeze, the perfect night for a walk into town. But was he ready to spend time walking so closely with Shelby? "I don't know, Cassidy. Maybe Miss Shelby isn't up to the long walk." He cringed inwardly. He'd made it sound like she was an invalid, or worse, that he didn't want her along.

"I'd welcome the walk. It's a lovely evening." Shelby smiled, a twinkle in her eye. "I don't mind if it's all right with you."

He shrugged and placed a hand on his son's shoulder. "Son, never argue when two females have spoken."

"Huh? What does that mean?"

"It means we're walking to town for pizza." He slipped his car keys back into his pocket and started toward the sidewalk. He tried to take a position beside his son as they walked, but the boy skipped ahead to be with his sister. That left him to fall in beside Shelby. He tensed, acutely aware of her at his side. It felt familiar, as natural as breathing. Memories from the past started to bloom, but he plucked them out like weeds. The past was over. It was the present he had to focus on. They'd walked nearly a block before she broke the silence.

"It's a lovely evening."

"Yes. It is."

"Thank you for inviting me. I know you'd rather have the kids to yourself tonight."

He glanced over at her, surprised at her perception. He had been looking forward to some close family time. "I'll have them all weekend. Besides, they like you. They wanted you to come, and you deserve a treat." He thought about Shelby living in that big old house alone. She must miss her grandmother. "Sorry Ellen had to leave town. I know you came home to spend time with her. Instead you're taking care of two ornery kids."

She smiled over at him. "She'll be home soon. My great-aunt is improving rapidly."

"Will you have time with her before you have to go back to New York?"

"We'll have time."

The tone in Shelby's voice made him look at her. She was staring straight ahead, making it hard to interpret her meaning. She never mentioned returning to New York. Odd given her devotion to her career. Was there something else keeping her in Dover besides her health and spending time with Ellen?

They walked in silence again, letting the children chatter up ahead. When they neared the edge of town, they stopped to wait for the traffic signal.

"I can't believe all the changes here since I left." Shelby smiled at him. "In many ways it's exactly as I remember. But in others, it's very different."

His heart skipped a beat. He focused on crossing the street and not the way her smile warmed his whole being. "It's grown a lot in the last ten years. The new auto plant brought in new business and new residents. It's been a good for Dover, and the people have developed a new attitude toward the history of the town.

There were a lot of people who hated our old buildings and old houses. But now they've embraced it. The state film commission has really marketed Dover to the movie industry."

"I know. *Magnolia Days*." She bounced slightly in delight. "I saw that movie three times. I was thrilled when I learned it was being shot on location here. It made me proud and a little homesick. I always thought this was one of the most charming towns in the whole state. No one has a town square as lovely as ours."

Matt wasn't sure he'd heard her right. "I thought you hated this place."

Shelby shot him a sheepish grin. "I thought I did, too."

"What changed your mind?"

She made a sweeping gesture with her hand. "I used to look at all those old buildings as walls trapping me in this backward place, preventing me from seeing the world beyond the old crumbling bricks."

"And now?"

She smiled and brushed her hair off her face. "Now I feel like it's a fence, keeping me safe. Like old friends giving me a warm hug each time I look at them."

His heart jumped in his chest. Was it possible she might actually consider staying? That was too outlandish a notion to even consider.

Shelby clasped her hands behind her back as they walked across the square. "I dreaded coming back. I expected to remember all the things I disliked about it. But since I've been here, it's the good memories that are resurfacing." She smiled over at him, lifting her shoulders in a slight shrug. "It actually feels good, comfortable to be here again. I was sure I'd feel lost after the pace of the big city, but this feels like home."

Matt forced his gaze forward and ignored the flutter in his chest that seemed to quicken whenever Shelby smiled at him. "I know what you mean. It was a big adjustment moving back after living in Atlanta, but I don't regret it. It's a good town, though we have our share of small minds and busybodies."

Shelby chuckled. "I've run into a few of them. The ones who can't understand why I left, and the ones who don't understand why I came back."

"I guess we never understand the decisions of others." He sensed Shelby stiffen.

"Probably not."

Did they understand each other? Things had been different between them since they'd declared their truce. Their relationship was less tense, more comfortable and friendly. He had to admit his resentment had eased. Even the wound of her rejection was healing over. The concern about her eventual departure and her health issues, however, remained. He was still sorting out his feelings about that.

Matt refilled his drink cup and turned around, catching sight of Shelby and his children huddled at the table, laughing. They looked like a family. He was the only one missing from the picture. When he sat down, anyone who glanced their way would assume they were a family. The idea sent a fist of pain into his gut. But they weren't. Shelby could never be part of the picture. His life was here. Hers was a thousand miles away. Something deep in his chest stirred, leaving him uneasy. He tried to shake off the feeling as he returned to the table, grateful for once that his daughter talked nonstop.

Kenny bit off a large hunk of pizza. "Can we play the games?"

Matt frowned. "Don't talk with your mouth full." He handed each child a few dollars. One of the things that made Angelo's so successful was the area in the back filled with an assortment of video and arcade games. The room was well supervised, and there was only one way in or out of the pizza parlor, so he didn't have to worry about their safety.

Matt watched his son and daughter dash off, only too aware that for the next half hour or so he and Shelby would be forced to converse alone. His earlier comment about understanding another's position had been replaying in his mind. He'd learned long ago to look for the positive in any situation, no matter how bad. He'd also learned that God really did make all things work for good.

He gathered his thoughts. "I owe you a debt of gratitude."

Shelby looked at him, a puzzled expression on her face. "It's not necessary. I enjoy watching the children and it helps fill up my days."

Matt shook his head. "I don't mean that. I mean—" He glanced out the window, gauging his words. "Leaving the way you did taught me a lot."

Shelby stared down at her glass, her fingers tracing lines in the condensation. "I'm sorry."

He was saying this all wrong. "No. You taught me things while we were together." He hesitated again. "I'll admit my attitude when I went back to college was to prove that I wasn't small-town."

"Matt—"

"I came to see that you'd shown me how to think outside the box. I guess your creativity rubbed off on me. It was probably the reason for my success as a businessman." He shrugged. "In an odd way, I owe a lot to you."

"I don't know what to say to that."

Matt wiped his palm across his jaw. "That didn't come out right." He turned to face her. "I guess what I'm trying to tell you is that God took my anger and resentment toward you and used it to make me a better businessman." He sighed. "I'm sorry if that came out as a backhanded compliment."

"No. I understand." A small smile moved her lips. "I was angry and resentful, too. I was determined to excel in school and go to work for a prestigious magazine the minute I graduated. And I did. The difference was, I didn't ask God for any help. I was sure I could do it all on my own. Until recently."

"What changed?"

Shelby looked away. "I hadn't counted on the stress factor."

Matt glanced down at her plate and the barely touched slice of vegetarian pizza. The heart thing. Her job must have been more hectic than he'd suspected. "Do you miss it? Your work?"

She shrugged, toying with her napkin. "Not as much as I'd expected to. To be honest, I don't know if I'll even have a job to go back to. The publisher I work for was bought out. No one knows yet exactly what that will mean for our futures, but probably layoffs and eliminations of most of our publications."

"I'm sorry, Shelby. That's tough." Matt's heart went out to her even as another piece of the puzzle fell into place. Shelby was staying here because she was out of work.

"My whole adult life has been focused on this job. Now it might all be gone."

"I get that. I loved my job, the company I built. But it took all my time and energy and there wasn't a lot left over for my family. I didn't want to sell, but neither did I want to ignore my kids. In the end, I'm much happier here in this new job than I ever would have imagined. Maybe you need to look in a new direction, too."

"That's what Gramma keeps telling me. Actually, I've been thinking about starting an online magazine. Something aimed at girls like Cassidy, only with a Christian focus."

Her idea surprised him. He'd seen a change in her on the outside, perhaps the bigger change was on the inside. Their situation, however, hadn't changed. Whether because of health or career, she would leave Dover sooner or later. "So, you'll be going back?"

"That's where all the publishers are." She stared out the window for a while then looked down at her plate.

Her tone lacked the conviction he'd heard in it previously. Was she changing her mind? Only a short time ago she'd admitted she felt at home here in Dover. Matt wondered if perhaps Shelby wasn't certain herself.

As the silence dragged on, Matt searched for a topic of conversation that didn't involve their past. He realized there wasn't one. She was ingrained with his past the way she was becoming part of his present. He glanced over at her, his gaze locking with hers. Was he crazy or was that affection he glimpsed in her brown eyes? Affection for him. The thought shook him.

Cassidy and Kenny skidded to a stop at Matt's side, forestalling any further small talk. "Can we have more money for the games?"

He shook his head. "Time to go."

Kenny's shoulders sagged, and he tilted his head backward in protest. "Aw. But I don't want to." A stern look from his father abruptly ended the whiny attitude.

"Then could we stop at the Picture Box and get a

movie? Please." Kenny clasped his fingers together like a little beggar.

Cassidy chimed in, "Please. It's Friday night. No school tomorrow."

Matt laid a tip on the table, then glanced at Shelby. She was smiling.

"Friday night movie night."

His mind snapped back to when he and Shelby were dating. Friday night was his night off and his brother's night to work in the store. It was the one night when he and Shelby could drive over to Sawyers Bend and catch a movie. They'd sit in the back, share a big bucket of popcorn and snuggle as close as the seat would allow.

"Miss Shelby could watch it with us, too."

The hopeful tone in his daughter's voice brought him back to the present. He started to kill the idea, then remembered she was alone in that big old house of Ellen's. "You're welcome to join us."

"Thank you, but I have some things to do at home. Maybe next time."

Was she telling the truth or was she remembering the past, as well, and not wanting to relive it?

Darkness was closing in quickly as they crossed the street and strolled through the park toward the far end of town. Matt again questioned his impulse in asking Shelby along tonight. Being around her always left him with a strange longing deep in his gut and wondering if kids and job were enough and if being alone was going to be his future.

He shook off the pointless speculation. Shelby could never be part of his future. She was all about career, not family. Her health issues were an obstacle he could never overcome. He glanced over at her and she smiled, sending a pinprick of guilt into his heart. Okay, that wasn't completely fair. She'd stepped into his life as if she'd always been there. As if she belonged. He'd been worried about her ability to manage two active kids. At times they were more than he could handle. But Shelby had taken charge like she was born to it. What would their lives have been like if things had turned out differently? It didn't matter. There were no do-overs in life. But there were second chances. If a person was willing to brave the dangers.

Was he ready to brave the dangers of loving again? Of risking the loss of someone he loved? Never! Yet he couldn't deny the longing he had to be part of a family again, a complete family. He couldn't ignore the ache inside that cried out for a wife to share his hopes and dreams and those of his children.

Matt turned back to Shelby. His throat thickened at the affection for his children displayed in her soft brown eyes. She'd always had a heart overflowing with love. He'd forgotten that. He'd forgotten many of the good things about their relationship.

As they continued strolling toward the gazebo, the lights flickered on, bathing the Victorian structure in a gentle light.

"Oh." Shelby exhaled softly. "I'd forgotten how beautiful it was."

Matt looked at the large ornate structure, then turned his gaze to Shelby. Her eyes were bright with happiness. Her brown hair was bathed in the glow from the light on the gazebo. The smile on her face was sweet and lovely and weakened his knees. He remembered a time when they had sat here late at night, talking about their future, holding each other. The memory was too real, too unexpected. Each moment he spent with her further weakened his barriers, and he couldn't afford to let that happen.

He was afraid it was too late.

Shelby let her gaze travel around the framework of the octagonal gazebo, memories resurfacing with each beat of her heart. Many times she'd come here alone to think when she didn't want to go home and face her mother's anger. Other times she'd come simply for the peace and quiet or to be with friends.

Her most cherished memories, however, centered around Matt. They'd often sit in here and talk about the life they would have together. As long as she could remember, she'd been marching toward college. Nothing and no one was going to get in her way. Until Matt. He'd taken her dreams to new levels, given her the courage to dream of things she'd never imagined before. He'd made her believe that together, they could do anything. It had all ended in a flash, leaving their love a pile of tiny shattered remnants.

They started forward again across the park and toward home. The walk home was quiet and thoughtful. Companionable. Shelby allowed herself to enjoy it while it lasted. What a mess. Everything was so complicated. Being near him again, caring for his children and getting involved with his daily life had only created turmoil in her own.

Each day she experienced an odd mixture of joy and despair when she entered Matt's home. The only things keeping her anchored were the comforting task of putting the scrapbook together and the steady resurfacing of her faith.

She had found another ray of sunshine in all of it. Thanks to Cassidy and Kenny, she'd discovered a nurturing side of herself she hadn't been aware of. She loved caring for them, and she liked being back home in Dover. But she relished putting the scrapbook together, as well. It brought back all the reasons she loved working for a magazine. She wasn't ready to give that up. Was it possible to have both? Did she even want both?

Yes. She did.

She glanced over at Matt. He was so close she could easily brush her hand against his arm. The thing that made it all so difficult was that she was still in love with him. She'd never stopped. But it was strictly one-sided, and that was all it would ever be. Even if he had feelings for her, there were too many barriers between them to take down. Her career and her past mistakes, but mostly her health. She couldn't expect him to take on that kind of uncertainty. It would be cruel.

Before she realized it they were home. The kids waved goodbye, and Matt walked with her to the door of Gramma's house. She turned to say good-night. Their eyes locked. For one fleeting moment, Shelby was eighteen again and seeing her future in a pair of navy blue eyes. She forced herself to think clearly. "Thank you for a lovely evening. I had a good time."

"Thank you for taking such good care of my son and daughter."

"You're welcome, but it's my pleasure." She braved another look into his eyes and saw the questions deep within, the lingering doubts. He was still wary of her health and of her return to New York. Two barriers that were too high to scale.

"Good night, Matt." Quickly she stepped back, digging her house key from her purse. Her shaky fingers refused to grasp it tightly, and it fell to the porch floor.

She reached to pick it up at the same moment as Matt. The contact knocked her off balance.

"Whoa." Matt grabbed her shoulders to steady her, and she smiled up at him. The look in his eyes froze her breath in her lungs. Her hand rested against the solid wall of his chest. His breath caressed her cheek. Time ceased. It was summer. They were young and in love. Shelby closed her eyes, her senses remembering every detail from long ago. The scent of him. The warmth of him. The tenderness.

"Shelby."

Her name whispered on his lips drew her eyes open. The look she saw reflected in his deep blue eyes was familiar. He lowered his head, lips slightly parted. Shelby trembled and closed her eyes, her heart singing. And then reality reared its ugly head. She couldn't let this happen. If they let old feelings cloud their judgment, both of them would be hurt. She pushed back, struggling to inhale. "It's late."

Matt stiffened. "Yeah." He bent down and picked up the key, handing it to her. He stared at her a moment, then walked down the steps and across the drive. It was over.

She'd never felt so alone in her whole life.

Chapter Eight

The knock came at the same instant Shelby touched the tip of the glue bottle to the back of the photograph. Letting out a puff of irritation, she quickly and carefully placed it on the page, trying to keep it centered.

Her new hobby had quickly become a passion and given her a special connection to Cassidy and Kenny as they worked on their scrapbook for their dad. The knock came again. Except of course when she was interrupted.

"I'm coming!" She scooted back her chair and trotted toward the front door, pulling it open. A surge of warm affection flowed through her when she recognized her visitor. "Laura Durrant."

"Hi, Shelby." The young woman opened her arms for a hug. "I'm so sorry it took me this long to come see you but I've been working over in Mobile."

Shelby held the hug an extra moment, basking in the warmth of her friendship. One of the joys of loving Matt had been the family that had come with him. Laura had been like the sister she'd never had.

"Come on in. I want to hear all about you." She led Laura to the sunroom, then brought iced tea and fruit to munch on. Once settled in they quickly covered the lost years.

"Okay," Shelby said a while later, after giving Laura a truncated version of her life story. "Enough about me. Tell me about you."

Laura accepted the refill on her glass of tea and picked up another apple slice. "Not much to tell."

"How did you end up running your own construction business? I thought you wanted to be an architect."

Laura stared at her glass a moment. "I did. I went to State, got my degree. Got a job in Houston. Met a guy and got married."

Shelby eyed her closely. From the tone of her voice there was much more to her story. "What happened?"

"He decided being married wasn't for him. He'd rather spend time with his buddies and enjoy a variety of lady friends." She shrugged. "Unlike you, I didn't adjust to big-city life very well. So I came home and bought this business from Mr. Olsen when he retired. We specialize in historic restoration projects."

"I've seen those trucks around town, but I had no idea they were yours. You must be doing really well."

Laura smiled. "So far so good. LC Construction is never out of work."

"Why the LC?"

She grinned and shrugged. "Laura Claire Constructions sounded too girlie. The initials were more professional."

Shelby couldn't fault her logic. "I see what you mean."

"So, are you coming to Mom and Dad's party tomorrow after church?"

"Oh, I'd like to, but I don't want to intrude."

Laura emitted a short grunt. "Don't be silly. You won't be. Didn't Matt invite you? He was supposed to."

Shelby took a bite of her apple slice, avoiding her friend's gaze. "Not exactly. The kids did. I think he went along with it not to be rude."

"Well, I'm inviting you. I know Mom and Dad would love to have you come. They've asked about you several times."

Her heart warmed. She'd expected them to view her as the villain in her relationship with their son. "I saw your dad the other day. I'm surprised he even remembers me."

Laura peered at her closely. "They loved you, Shelby. They expected you to be their daughter-in-law. We were all shocked and saddened when you two broke up. Don't misunderstand." Laura leaned forward to emphasize her point. "We all loved Katie, but we loved you, too."

"And I loved all of you. Things just didn't work between us. It wasn't meant to be, I guess."

"Well, that's all in the past. So will you come to the picnic? You can hang out with me if you'd like. Ignore that bullheaded brother of mine. Shiloh Lake is a big place."

Laura had a point. "Okay. I'd love to come."

"Good. Well, I have to go." Laura stood and opened her arms for another hug. "Don't be a stranger. We can be friends no matter what your relationship with my brother, you know."

Laura's visit had lifted Shelby's spirits. She'd always assumed that since she'd jilted Matt, the rest of his family hated her. It was wonderful to find she'd been wrong. She'd loved his whole family and had looked forward to being part of it. Laura's history had surprised her. She'd always assumed that other people's lives were perfect, that hers was the only one filled with trouble. But Matt had lost his wife. Laura had endured a failed marriage. Yet both had found new purpose and new focus in their lives. Even her friend Pam had managed to achieve her goals.

Being back in Dover was opening her eyes to a lot of things and giving her a new perspective about possibilities she'd never considered. What other paths in her life had she missed because she'd been focused on one way with no thought of the alternatives?

Maybe there was something beyond *Tween Scene*. Maybe the door closing on Harmon Publishing would open a new door someplace else. A job with less stress, with more time for a personal life. But she'd never know if she didn't try. A good place to start would be updating her résumé. She was well respected in the business; her reputation was good. Surely there were other companies who would welcome her job skills and experience.

With her determination renewed, she picked up her laptop and headed outside to the patio in the backyard. The weather was beautiful. She'd forgotten how sweet an autumn afternoon in Dover could feel. She'd work awhile then maybe she'd call Pam and see if she'd like to have lunch or go shopping.

After settling into the cushioned lounge chair she started to work, pulling up her résumé and then listing contacts that she could query. She'd been working for some time when she noticed the fan in her laptop was running unusually hard. The computer grew hot on her thighs. She lifted it to allow some airflow underneath. Her fingers brushed the underneath panel. It was hot. Too hot. The fan whined louder.

The heat increased, scalding her skin below her denim shorts. She screamed, shoving the computer to the ground as it burst into flames. Helpless, she watched as the flames crawled over the keyboard and up the screen. "Oh, no. No! Help!"

Someone appeared at her side, pulling her a safe distance from the small fire, which was now burning itself out.

"What happened?"

She shook her head, realizing Matt was at her side. "I don't know. I was working and it got hot. Then it burst into flames." Her laptop was now a blackened, charred mess.

"Are you all right?" He took her hands in his and inspected them. "No burns?"

She pulled them away and touched her thighs. They looked red but not burned. "No. But look at my laptop." She sighed and turned away from the smoking debris. "It's my own fault. I should have taken it back."

"What do you mean?"

"I got a recall notice about the faulty battery over a year ago. I never found time to take it in to be replaced."

"Do you have backup files?"

An inventory of her files scrolled across her mind. The lost information, personal and work related, could never be regained. "I back up all my files on a company system. I can probably access them when I get back." Unless of course there was no reason to go back. The files might be pointless soon.

"What about your personal information?"

She became aware of Matt's hand resting on her lower back, offering steady comfort. She focused on his question only to realize with a sinking heart that there were precious few personal items on her computer to worry about. No pictures to speak of that didn't involve work events, no pets, no real friends. Not even boring travel photos. Tears welled up again. What a sad, lonely life she had. She tried but couldn't stop the sobs that erupted from her chest. Matt held her closer, which didn't help at all.

"Shelby?"

The concern in his voice, the tenderness, was her undoing. She turned into his chest and let the tears fall. His arms enfolded her, chasing away the fear and giving her a safe place to fall.

He made soft soothing sounds, holding her tightly until she ran out of tears. She stepped back, swiping away the tears on her cheeks. "I'll be fine."

"Is there anything I can do?" He reached out and gently brushed her hair off her forehead.

She gestured toward the charred computer. "Can you fix it?"

Matt laughed out loud. "I don't think so. It's pretty much done for."

She frowned and rested her head against his shoulder.

"Come on over to the house. I want to take a look at that burn. You need something on that."

She started to protest, but it had started to sting. In fact it was becoming downright uncomfortable. Meekly she followed him across the drive and into his house. He set her down at the kitchen table, then went to retrieve the first aid supplies.

He stooped down in front of her, steadying her leg with one strong hand and applying the ointment with the other. The contact sent a different kind of quiver up her spine.

"This'll be sore for a few days. Keep the ointment on it and it should heal quickly."

Her gaze drifted to the crown of his head and the thick wavy hair. She could reach out and run her fin-

gers through it with only a slight movement. If only...
He stood, smiling down at her.

"I think you'll live. Are you feeling better?"

All she could manage was a nod.

"Sorry about the computer, Shelby, but I'm glad you weren't seriously hurt."

"Me, too. I never expected to be set on fire by my laptop."

Matt smiled, holding up his hand as if he'd just gotten an idea. "I know what will make you feel better."

He moved to the cupboard, pulled something out, then went to the microwave and placed it inside. In a few moments, the aroma of popcorn filled the kitchen. She had to smile. He remembered. It was their preferred snack. Popcorn and movies. When they couldn't go to the theater in Sawyers Bend, they would put in a DVD and watch it in the den at Matt's. She smiled over at him. He looked quite pleased with himself. "You're right. It will make me feel better."

She realized suddenly that the house was very quiet. "Where are Cassidy and Kenny?"

Matt took the bag of popped corn from the microwave and dumped it into a bowl. "Turns out that party Kenny had today was for Molly's little brother. They live up the street, so Cassidy went along to help play hostess. I have a rare day alone in my own house."

"Until you had to play rescuer."

"I'm glad I was here to help."

"Cassidy will make a great hostess."

He snickered and sat down. "You mean because she's so bossy?"

She had to chuckle. "True, but it's good she likes to take charge. She'll be a good leader someday."

"Well, we'll see. She's a challenge at times. I wonder if I'm doing the right things."

"You're a great dad, Matt."

Matt ran a hand down the back of his neck, a doubtful smile on his face. "I don't know about that. I'm afraid I'm getting into dangerous territory."

"What do you mean?"

"Cassidy." He shook his head. "She's changing before my eyes. Physically and emotionally she's becoming a young woman, and I'm finding it harder to connect with her. She really needs her mother now."

Shelby ached for him. "You'll do fine. And you have your mom here, and Laura. They'll help you."

Matt nodded. "They do, but I worry that she doesn't have someone around to guide her, someone she can confide in. I'd like to think she'd talk to me about girl things, but I know that's not realistic."

"I don't know if that's necessarily true." She took a bite of popcorn, reminding herself to go easy on the salty treat. "I had a friend who found it easier to talk to her dad than her mom. Have a little faith. It'll all work out." She reached over and laid her hand on his and felt him tense.

She pulled her hand away and prepared to go. "I've taken enough of your quiet time for today. I appreciate you coming to my aid. I guess I'd better go toss that computer in the trash."

Matt stood and walked her to the door. "Leave it. I'll pick it up after it's cooled down and take it to the recycling station."

"Thanks." His eyes locked on her again, and she wished she could know what he was thinking. Then again, maybe not.

* * *

Matt shoved his chair back from the computer desk and stood. He'd been staring at the same screen, the same sentences for ten minutes, unable to concentrate. For the first time in months he had quiet time to catch up on paperwork and he couldn't get thoughts of Shelby out of his mind. Her reaction to the computer fire nagged at him. She'd cried. He couldn't recall a time when he'd seen her break down that way. Granted, it had been a terrifying experience. But the Shelby he remembered would have fussed and fumed, given the offending device a swift kick and gone out and bought a new one. Instead she'd succumbed to tears and, even more surprising, allowed him to comfort her.

He'd never seen her so vulnerable. Was her heart issue the cause? He'd never stopped to consider it from her point of view. Suddenly faced with walking away from her career, forced to change her way of life, with the threat of another, more serious heart attack hanging over her. It couldn't have been easy, not to mention frightening.

Matt rubbed his jaw. Her reaction wasn't the only thing gnawing at his mind. He couldn't shake the very physical memory of holding her in his arms, cradled against his heart. The closeness still vibrated through him like lightning, bringing every molecule in his body to tingling life. He'd wanted to protect her, to shelter her from any harm.

He had to face the fact that he was losing his heart to Shelby all over again. And that was a very unwise thing to do. It wasn't simply his own feelings at stake but those of his children, too. And at the root of it all was the nagging question of why she'd walked out on him fifteen years ago. What had gone wrong? What had changed so suddenly?

One day they were engaged. The next she'd thrown the ring in his face. He'd been over it a thousand times in his head, trying to remember something he'd missed. All he remembered was that from the moment he'd met her, he'd known she was the one he wanted to spend his future with.

Meeting her had changed his life. He'd been filled with resentment and irritation over missing out on his sophomore year of college. His father had been seriously injured in an automobile accident and Matt had been needed to help run the store. Initially he'd been more than willing to do his part for the family. But one semester had stretched into two, and he'd grown more and more dissatisfied. Then his mom had hired Shelby to work for the summer and everything had changed. Until the night she'd walked away and left his heart bleeding. He'd never heard from her again.

Allowing himself to fall for her a second time would be insanity. He had to remember they were only friends and that she was doing him a favor. Reliving the past, allowing those old feelings to be rekindled, would only hurt them both. The past was best forgotten.

Shelby carried her mug out to the front porch the next morning and sat on the swing. For the first time since arriving in Dover, she wasn't obsessing over her future or Matt living next door. She took a sip of her coffee and smiled. It didn't taste so bad today. The house was empty without Gramma, but time alone was a good thing. She had a lot to think about, a lot of soul-searching to do. She and the Lord had come to terms last night. She'd released her stranglehold on her life and given it over to Him. During her reading, she'd been reminded that there was a time for everything, and at this point in her life, everything had been torn down and it was time to build it up again.

The gentle movement of the swing soothed her. She became aware of birds singing in the trees overhead, the breeze stirring the dark leaves on the live oak in the yard. Sunlight filtered through the fading leaves splattered over the ground, and the air held the faintest hint of autumn.

So this is what it meant to be free of stress. To be calm and peaceful. She didn't think she'd ever known this kind of contentment before. She liked it. She'd been running from her past, running from her fears, running from her mistakes so long, she'd forgotten how to stop and rest and it had almost killed her. It might still if she didn't learn to make significant changes in her life.

Glancing down at the red spot on her leg, she gently probed the edge. It felt much better today. It had been tender and sore. Thanks to Matt's gentle ministrations it was going to heal quickly. His thoughtfulness had only made her love him more. Being friends again had given her a sense of peace and joy. But Matt had been deeply wounded by his wife's death and had no intention of risking his heart or those of his children again. She would never ask him to. Even with all her lifestyle changes, her heart disease would be an ongoing concern in her life.

Today, however, she would concentrate on enjoying the time she had left. Time with Matt and the children, time in her hometown and soon time with Gramma. Her great-aunt was recovering quickly, and Gramma would be coming home soon. She'd worry about tomorrow when it got here.

Chapter Nine

For the first time in a long while, Shelby was actually looking forward to something. The anniversary picnic for the Durrants was today. The whole town of Dover was filled with excitement, and she wanted to be a part of it. Not only for Tom and Angie Durrant, but she wanted to reconnect with her hometown and become part of the community again. A notion she was still trying to process.

She was looking forward to seeing Matt and the children, too. She hadn't seen them at church that morning. They probably had gone to the early service so they could help set up the picnic.

Sliding her feet into a pair of comfortable sandals, she walked to the mirror and assessed her clothing choices. She'd opted for a denim skirt and a print blouse. Capri pants and a comfy T-shirt might have been more practical, but she wanted to look feminine today. She didn't want to examine the reasons why. Best just go and not think about it.

Shelby walked toward the Shiloh Lake picnic grounds a short while later, smiling at the number of people already filling the parking lot and milling around the grounds. A large banner was strung between two trees, proclaiming the event. Clusters of colorful balloons bracketed each end of the sign welcoming the guests. The Durrant family was beloved in Dover and she understood, better than most, why.

They were the embodiment of the Dover motto: Faith, Friends, Family. They cared about their community and about each other. They could always be counted on to lend a hand or a prayer. She'd always envied the close relationship she'd observed in Matt's family. They laughed and joked with each other, and genuinely enjoyed each other's company. It was a life she longed for, a life she'd dreamed about. But one she'd never known personally.

Stepping beneath the banner, she glanced around for a familiar face. To her right, a row of grills and cookers had been set up. The delicious aromas wafting toward her made her stomach growl. She knew from experience that the fare would include everything from hot dogs and burgers to chicken, ribs and fish. No one would leave here hungry.

To her left she saw a long table decorated with ribbons. And more balloons. An assortment of gifts covered the top. She walked toward it and added her own present to the mounting pile—the small wheel of flavored pecans. Something she remembered Matt's parents liked.

"Hey, Shel." Pam Fleming touched her shoulder. "Glad to see you made it. I want you to meet my family."

Shelby greeted her husband, whom she remembered from high school, and their three children, the oldest one a strapping teenage boy.

"You're welcome to sit with us."

"I might do that, but first I want to speak to the Durrants."

Pam pointed them out, seated near the edge of the lake. Before Shelby could move, Cassidy waved and ran to meet her. "I didn't think you were ever going to get here."

She smiled, giving her a hug.

"Will you sit with us? Please, please?"

She'd like nothing better. "Sure, but first I want to say hello to your grandparents." Cassidy held her hand as they made their way through the picnic grounds and to the wooden bench where the couple appeared to be holding court. The years had been kind to the couple. Mr. Durrant was a bit thinner, gray around the temples, but still lean and energetic. Matt would no doubt resemble him as he aged. Mrs. Durrant was grayer as well, her hair cut short and her figure a little softer in spots, but her smile was as lovely and warm as ever. A perfect match to her sweet spirit. She was the kind of woman Shelby would like to become.

Angie Durrant rose and greeted her like a long-lost daughter. "Shelby. It is so good to see you again. Not a day has gone by that I haven't thought about you and prayed for you."

Shelby was touched beyond words. She ached for all she'd thrown away. "That is so sweet. I really appreciate that. I need lots of prayers at the moment."

"How are you doing? Tom tells me you are battling some health issues."

"I'm fine. Truly. I just need to take better care of myself. It's nothing serious."

"Good. I hope those grandkids of mine aren't wearing you out. I know I have trouble keeping up with them."

"Not at all. In fact, they were just the remedy I needed. I love watching Cassidy and Kenny. They are delightful."

Angie Durrant touched her arm gently. "Well, I'm so very grateful that you were here to step in and take charge when Matt needed help. I hated that I couldn't come to his rescue, but with this campaign in full swing I just didn't have the time. And remember, if you should need us, for any reason, don't hesitate to call."

"Thank you, I won't."

"Come sit here and tell me all about yourself." Mrs. Durrant patted the bench beside her. Shelby sat down, and Tom and Angie leaned toward her, as if enclosing her into their circle. A lump rose unexpectedly in her throat. If things had turned out differently, these dear people would have been her in-laws.

She'd finished telling the Durrants about the scrapbooking she was doing when Tom Durrant glanced up and smiled.

"Matt, my boy. Why don't you escort Shelby here over to that food table? We've been monopolizing all her time. She must be starving."

She looked up at him, surprised to find a friendly sparkle in his deep blue eyes. "I guess he heard my stomach rumbling."

Matt held out his hand to help her up. "Then follow me. I can get you to the head of the line. I haven't eaten yet myself."

Matt fell in beside her, matching his stride to her shorter one. Shelby tried not to remember how often they had done this, how much she missed it. His hand was so close it would only take a slight movement to slip her fingers into his. "Looks like you had a good turnout. I think everyone in town is here."

"Probably so. My parents know everyone. I think that's why Mom wanted a picnic instead of a formal party. This was a lot easier."

"It suits them, too. Your parents were never the pretentious type."

"No, they're not. They've always been more at home in a park than a country club. How's your leg?"

She slowed and glanced downward. Her skirt ended right above the fading red spot. "Almost all healed up. Maybe you should have been a doctor."

Matt chuckled. "No, I don't think so. Too squeamish. I can't handle being around sick people."

Silence settled over them again, looming like a shadow. Like a woman with heart disease. When they reached the food table, Shelby picked up a plate and started down the line of sumptuous dishes. Matt followed, making conversation with several others as they filed along the food line. When their plates were heaping full, they took them to a table nestled near a large, sprawling magnolia tree. Shelby had tried to remember to make healthy choices, but it was difficult. Hopefully she'd get better as time when on. Matt went back for their drinks then sat down, eyeing her plate.

"You planning on eating all of that?"

Was he worried she wasn't taking care of herself? Out of concern for his children of course. The twinkle in his eyes eased her mind. "Not all of it. But it's been a long time since I've had picnic food. I want to at least taste most of it. But only one bite of each. Then I'll have to double up on the exercise tomorrow."

"Don't they have picnics in New York?"

"Of course. In fact they have a Mississippi Day in Central Park. I just never had the time to attend." Shelby took a bite of potato salad and released an audible moan of satisfaction, all thoughts of Matt and his motives vanishing. "This has to be Mrs. Johnson's."

Matt chuckled. "Oh yeah. No one makes potato salad like she does."

Shelby swallowed with difficulty. It was nice to hear him laugh again. They'd found so much to laugh at that summer. Merely being together had created joy.

Cassidy and Kenny skidded to a stop at the edge of the table, stalling her train of thought.

"Can we have ice cream now?" Cassidy pleaded. "Darcy's mom brought some triple chocolate chip."

Matt nodded. "Go ahead. But don't blame me if you have a stomachache tonight."

A few moments later the children were back. Cassidy sat beside her father. Kenny climbed in next to her. Her heart ached. With little effort she could envision this as her family. She glanced at Matt, surprised to find him studying her. There was an odd look in his blue eyes. Not angry or disapproving but more assessing. It made her uncomfortable.

"Tell us about you and Shelby and what y'all did in the olden days," Cassidy asked with a huge smile.

Shelby laughed.

Matt frowned. "Olden days?"

"Yeah, back when you were in school. Gramma said Shelby worked at the store. Did you?"

"I did." She pushed her paper plate aside. "I started after graduation and worked until I went to college that fall." The last period in her life she wanted to revisit at the moment.

"What did you do at my grandpa's store?" Kenny wondered. "Did you fix stuff?"

"No." She chuckled. "I was a salesclerk."

"Were you two an item?" Cassidy propped her chin on her fists and smiled in anticipation.

Matt groaned softly. Shelby decided to rescue him. "We were friends."

"Good friends?"

Shelby laughed. "Yes. We'd hang out on weekends. You know, the usual stuff. Movies. Burgers. When the weather was nice, we'd hop on his bike and ride around the countryside."

"What kind of bike?" Kenny asked, resting his elbows on the table and staring at her with interest.

She had to chuckle at the boy's curiosity. He was such an adorable, lovable child, she had to fight to keep from hugging him all the time. "A motorcycle."

"You had a motorcycle?" Cassidy gaped at her father in stunned amazement.

Matt nodded, a serious expression on his face. "That was back in the olden days. The days before time was invented."

"Cool." Kenny's voice was filled with awe and respect. "What happened to it?"

Shelby found herself wondering the same thing. Judging by the kids' reaction, Matt had given up riding long ago.

"Your mother didn't think it was safe, so I sold it." He smiled down at his daughter. "I didn't want to worry her."

Cassidy leaned against Matt's shoulder, a huge smile on her face. "Were you one of those biker dudes with big boots and a leather jacket and a bandana?"

Matt grimaced. "No. Where do you get these ideas?"

"Where did you go, Daddy? Did you ride all over the mountains and stuff like I see on TV?"

Shelby's heart tightened with a sweet ache. Those

days with Matt were some of her most cherished memories. She didn't visit them much; it was too painful. But sharing them here and now with Matt's children made it enjoyable again.

"No," Matt replied with a smile. "We only rode around here. Sometimes we'd go to Jackson, and one time we drove down to the coast."

Cassidy rolled her eyes. "Boring."

"Oh, I don't know." Matt held Shelby's gaze. "I remember a trip to Brookhaven and a certain farmer who might disagree."

Shelby blinked. She couldn't believe he remembered that, let alone brought it up. "We're lucky he didn't have us arrested."

"What did you do?" Cassidy demanded, all ears. Kenny's eyes were wide with fascination.

"I think you'd better ask your father." Far be it from her to be the one to tell tales to his kids.

Matt grinned and shook his head. "Let's say we wandered a little too far off the road and ended up in the wrong place at the wrong time."

"Aw, come on. Tell us."

Two pairs of little eyes stared at her expectantly. Shelby chuckled with the memory. "I'll tell you we were covered in mud. It took me days to get it out of my hair. His leather jacket was ruined."

Cassidy poked her dad with her fingers. "I knew it. You did have a leather jacket. But I can't see you riding a big old bike. Too weird."

"Well, I did. Guess that was in my wilder days."

Cassidy giggled. "You? Wild? Prove it. You got any pictures?"

"No."

Shelby looked over at Matt. He'd responded too

quickly. Did he still have some of those photos? She found that hard to believe. He had never been the type to keep mementos. But oh how she wished he had kept a few. It would mean that somewhere deep inside he still cared.

"Do you have any?" Cassidy asked, looking at Shelby expectantly.

"No. Sorry. I'm sure my mom threw out all my stuff when she got married and moved away." That wasn't completely true. She had a couple photos, but they were packed away and hadn't been seen or even thought about in years.

"Shelby Russell, is that you?" A woman approached the picnic table, a huge smile on her face.

Matt grabbed the opportunity to excuse himself. He wandered off a short distance, tossing his half-empty plate into the trash can. He glanced back at Shelby chatting with her old friend.

His children sat across the picnic table, listening intently. After a few minutes, the friend walked off and Shelby turned her attention back to the kids. They all laughed, talking animatedly. An odd longing tugged at his heart. He turned away from the sight and glanced around the large park. Was it his imagination or was everyone here a couple?

He rarely thought about being single. As a widower, he was too busy with the kids, his job, his ministry. No time to worry about himself. But he'd be lying if he didn't admit he missed having someone at his side. He'd felt the emptiness more strongly over the last few weeks. Since Shelby had come home.

His gaze traveled once again to Shelby. The children were rising from the table, probably going off to the playground. Kenny stopped and gave Shelby a hug before dashing off like a small rocket. A smile lit Shelby's face as his daughter blew her a kiss before hurrying after her brother. Her gaze drifted toward him, stopping as their eyes met. A cold finger of loneliness traced across his senses and into his heart. He longed for companionship again, but the risks were too high. The pain of loss was too great to chance ever again.

He broke eye contact and turned away. He couldn't allow a moment's loneliness to cloud the issues. Cassidy and Kenny were all that mattered. They'd been devastated by Katie's death. Both had suffered serious depression, nightmares and illness. It had taken all he had, and God's grace, to get them through the grieving process.

Still, he worried sometimes about what they were missing by not having a mother. A mother who would hug them, guide them and laugh with them the way Shelby did. He glanced back at the table. Shelby had left. He caught sight of her walking toward the lake. Alone. Maybe he should join her.

"There you are, dear. Laura wants a family picture. You're the only one missing." His mother slipped her arm in his. "Except Tyler, of course. I wish he could get home more."

"Me, too." Ty had called last night to say he wouldn't make it home after all. The case he was working was coming to a head and he needed to see it through. Matt walked with his mom to the arbor, where his father waited. Laura had somehow lured Cassidy and Kenny back from the playground. He had the sudden impression that Shelby should be here, part of the picture.

Once the photograph was taken, his gaze immediately searched out Shelby. He found her standing with her friend Pam and another woman, sharing a laugh. For someone who professed a love of the big city, she fit perfectly into small-town life. For a moment he allowed himself to remember his old dreams. Shelby was supposed to have been part of his life, to have shared all its joys and the triumphs. Instead, she'd chosen her love for her career over her love for him.

He needed to accept the fact that he might never know why. And even if he did, it wouldn't change a thing. Matt turned when he heard his name called, raising his hand in greeting as a friend approached. "Hey, Dave. Glad you could make it." Dave was the local dentist and a good friend of his sister, Laura.

"Me, too. It's a great shindig. We're getting up a game of family volleyball. Get the kids and join us. We're setting up over in the far field."

"Sounds like fun. Thanks."

Matt searched out Shelby again. She had left her friend and was once again with his children, He started forward to recruit them for the volleyball game. Family volleyball. But they weren't really a family. So why did he keep thinking of them that way?

Shelby finished the piece of fruit on her plate and sighed. It had been a wonderful day. She'd been able to set aside all her worries and simply enjoy each moment. She'd played volleyball with Matt and the children. With parents and children all playing together it had been a pretty tame competition, which kept her lack of athletic ability from being exposed. She'd renewed a few old acquaintances and thoroughly enjoyed herself.

The afternoon sun was giving way to twilight, and the picnic was winding down. The grills had been loaded back onto their trucks, the food cleared away and the extra lawn chairs folded and carted off. She was sad to see the day end.

"Bye, Miss Shelby. We'll see you tomorrow." Kenny waved and hurried to her side.

She rested her hand on his waist and smiled. "Yes, you will. Are you leaving?"

Laura Durrant joined them. "I told them we could go watch a movie at my place. I thought it might let them calm down a bit. They're totally wound up."

Cassidy shook her head. "No, we're not."

"Oh yes, you are," Matt chimed in. "Behave yourselves. I'll pick you up after the movie."

Once they were gone, Shelby stood and smiled at Matt. "I guess I'd better be going, too. I had a good time today."

"Me, too. I hate to see it end. Would you like to take a walk along the lake for a few minutes?"

The idea was tempting. Spending time with him was always on her wish list. "Sure."

They started across the wide grassy area toward the water's edge and the well-worn path along the bank, walking in companionable silence, with only the sound of nature filling the cool, quiet air.

"It's so beautiful here."

"Yes, it is. We used to come here often to walk along this path. Do you remember?"

She stole a quick glance at him. His chiseled features were relaxed, free of the worry she so frequently saw. "I do."

He slowed and stepped off the path, walking toward a large live oak, its branches draped in thick strands of Spanish moss. "Do you remember this?"

She moved closer, her heartbeat racing as she recognized the large heart and the pair of initials carved inside. SR + MD. "Our tree. I'd forgotten about this." She glanced upward to the branches. "It's so much bigger than I remembered."

"It's been fifteen years. Things change."

She traced the heart with her fingers. "Yes, they do. Many things change." A small chuckle rose up from inside. She turned and smiled at him. "I remember the day you did this. You must have planned ahead because you had one of those battery-operated carving tools with you. The kind your dad sold in the store."

Matt chuckled. "I remember."

"You said you wanted it to last forever so everyone could see it when they passed by."

Matt leaned against the trunk and placed his fingers beside the heart. "Looks like it did for the most part. The tree has grown around some of it."

She could see he had something on his mind. "Matt, why did you bring me here?" He was silent a long moment, as if searching for the right words.

"I want to sort things out in my head. About you. About us. I thought maybe we could settle some of them."

Her throat tightened. Was he putting an end to her babysitting? Asking her to step out of his life? "All right. Maybe it would be for the best."

He faced her, a deep frown creasing his forehead. "What happened that night? Why did you suddenly change your mind about us? One day you're accepting my ring and then the next suddenly I'm too small-town."

Shelby bit her lip, trying to find a good place to start. She ignored the quickening of her heart. They needed to have this out, but it wasn't going to be easy. "Because you changed the plan."

Matt shook his head, puzzled. "What plan? The only plan I had was to marry you."

"Yes, but not until after college." Shelby ran a hand over her arm and turned away, putting distance between them. His confusion hovered between them like the moss dangling overhead.

Matt exhaled in exasperation. "Right. So?"

"I didn't want to give up my education and stay here in Dover. That wasn't the plan we always talked about."

He ran a hand down the back of his neck. "Shelby, I know how important your education was to you. I'd never have asked you to give that up." He paced off a few steps. "None of this is making any sense."

She took a few steps toward him, anxious for him to understand. "When I met you at the gazebo that night you told me you didn't think you were going back to college. You said you'd missed so much already because of your dad's accident that you might as well take over the store. Then you started talking about what a great life your parents had, how owning the store would let us start a family sooner."

"Yeah. I remember, but I was just talking, Shelby. Dad's relapse had thrown everything into chaos. With him back in the hospital, not knowing if he'd survive another surgery, my future was looking pretty bleak. I'd been counting on going to school the next week and then it was all taken away again." He exhaled a heavy sigh. "That night I was angry and confused. I had to face reality. If my dad didn't pull through, I'd be the head of the family. I'd have to take over the store and finishing college would be out of the question." He looked into her eyes, a sad smile on his handsome face. "I guess I was trying to hold on to the one sure thing in my life at the time. You. Us."

Shelby looked over at him, her heart aching. "I didn't know your dad had gone back into the hospital. Why didn't you tell me?"

"I did. I told your mom when I called and left the message for you to meet me."

Shelby quickly sorted through her memories of that day. She'd been troubled about a lot of things. Her mom hadn't been at all happy about the engagement. And she'd just learned her friend Pam, who was supposed to be her roommate at college, was pregnant and getting married instead. "She never mentioned it to me."

"Why would she not tell you? Did she dislike me that much?"

"It wasn't you in particular. It was anything that might tempt me away from school. She was furious when I came home with your ring on my finger. She was determined that I would have a better life than she had, and she didn't think you'd ever be more than the next owner of a small-town hardware store." She stared at the heart carved in the tree trunk. "So when you started talking about taking over the store, I guess I panicked." She braved a look at Matt, but could read only confusion in his eyes. She tried to explain further. "The ring suddenly became a chain and I had to break it."

"So you ran away without a word."

Shelby nodded. "Mom was relieved when I told her I'd broken up with you. She gave me money to leave for school early. I left the next morning."

"That's what your mom told me when I came by the house the next day looking for you. I didn't want to believe you'd do that." He held her gaze. "I called and I wrote to you, but you never answered so I finally got the message. We were through."

"I never got any letters. Or phone calls."

Matt shook his head. "I called your cell phone two or three times a day."

Shelby rubbed the tension between her eyes. "I didn't have a cell phone."

"You must have. Your mom gave me the number and your address at school." He touched his temple as if calling up a memory. "Someplace on Belmont Street."

A sinking sensation formed inside her. "I never lived on a street by that name. Ever."

"Why would your mother deliberately give me bogus information?"

"To ensure I got out of Dover and got the education she never had."

Shelby's gaze locked with Matt's. The realization of what had occurred changed everything. To a point.

His voice was rough, tinged with regret when he spoke. "I should have tried harder."

"I should have reached out to you." Shelby's heart ached with the sadness of it all. She moved to the trunk and touched the carved heart again. "Things could have been so different."

Matt moved toward her. "It's not good to dwell in the past, Shelby. Things happen for a reason. We both moved on. I have my family. You have your career. Those are good things. I guess it was just the wrong time for us."

Shelby looked up into his blue eyes, her heart filled with love for this man. "Is there a right time?"

He reached out and touched a stray hair near her temple. "A do-over?"

She nodded, unable to take her gaze from his. The deep blue darkened as he gazed into her eyes. His hand came up and rested against the side of her face, and she tilted her head into his palm.

"I hope so."

His words were spoken so softly she was certain she'd heard them only in her heart. Matt's strong hands gripped her shoulders, drawing her closer. She thought he was going to kiss her, but instead he pulled her against his chest, wrapping her in his warm embrace. Neither one spoke or moved.

A part of Shelby's heart that had long been scarred began to heal. Nothing could change the past, but now they could finally put it behind them. Slowly, Matt released her, taking her hand in his. They walked from under the old oak and back toward the park.

Shelby curled up in her bedroom chair, flipping through a magazine. It was late and she should be in bed, but she was reluctant to see the day come to an end. She was pleasantly tired and relaxed. A good feeling. Nothing like the exhaustion she normally knew after a busy day at work. She'd come home, showered, had a light meal and called her grandmother.

The Durrants' picnic had been more enjoyable than she'd anticipated. She'd expected to feel uncomfortable, out of synch with the people there. Instead she'd felt very much a part of it all. Like she belonged in Dover.

But mostly her thoughts centered around Matt. It felt good to finally clear away the past. What a mess. The perfect storm of bad circumstances. She could see clearly now how her fear coupled with her mother's meddling had cost her the thing she wanted most. She'd spent the rest of her life trying to replace it with her career.

So what would her relationship with Matt be now? Being held in his arms had torn away the flimsy curtain protecting her emotions. Her love for him was as deep and as strong as the day he'd given her his ring. But no one could go back and redo the past. He'd said he hoped they had a second chance, but he'd probably meant as friends. Anything else was impossible.

The phone rang. She rose and quickly moved to the nightstand. It was nearly eleven. Who would be calling at this hour?

"Hello."

"Shelby, I'm sorry to call so late."

"Matt?" His voice was tense, filled with a frightening urgency.

"I need you to come over here."

"What happened? Are the children all right?" Fear sent a paralyzing jolt through her system. She couldn't bear it if anything happened to Cassidy or Kenny.

"Yes. It's Ty. He's been shot. Mom and Dad are trying to get a flight out to Dallas to be with him. I need to take them to the airport in Jackson. They're both too upset to drive. Can you come over and stay with the kids?"

"Of course. I'll be there in five minutes."

"Thanks."

Shelby hung up, her heart aching for Matt and his family. His brother Ty was her age. They'd graduated from high school the same year. She hadn't known him well. He'd worked at the store the summer she did, but Ty had worked when Matt was off so she'd had little opportunity to get to know him. She sent up a prayer for Ty. She couldn't begin to imagine what Mr. and Mrs. Durrant must be going through.

She dressed quickly and hurried across the driveway. Matt yanked open the door before she could knock. He looked distracted. Lines of worry bracketed his mouth, and his blue eyes were darker than usual.

"Thanks, Shelby." He motioned her inside. "The kids are asleep. I haven't told them anything. I'll do that when I know more. I don't know how long I'll be gone." He rubbed his forehead and glanced around the room. "I need to get to Mom and Dad's. They're frantic."

Shelby's heart ached for him. He was rambling. Trying to think of every detail. She reached out and touched his arm. "Matt. Don't worry about anything here. We'll be fine. Go do what you have to."

"Yeah."

He looked so distraught she wanted to hold him, but that was out of the question. Instead she put a smile on her face and gestured toward the door. "Go. I'll be fine."

Matt pulled out his keys and started for the door. "Oh. In case I'm not back, the kids have to get up around six-thirty to get ready for school."

Shelby put her hands on his chest, intending to turn him toward the door. To her shock Matt laid his hand over hers. "Thank you, Shelby. I don't know what I'd do without you."

She smiled, her heart beating triple time. "That's what friends are for."

His eyes softened, and he touched her cheek with his fingers. "I guess so."

He turned and went out the door. Leaving a fluttering of hope in her heart. Maybe he still cared a little. Slowly she shut the door, knowing that friendship would be a poor substitute for her real feelings. But she would take what she could get and be grateful.

Chapter Ten

It was midmorning the next day before Matt had a chance to slow down and regroup. He poured a second cup of coffee from the pot on his credenza, then sat down at his desk. He was beat. It had been after four in the morning when he'd finally gotten back home from Jackson-Evers Airport. He and Shelby had exchanged only a few words when he'd returned. He'd had nothing new to report on his brother's condition, and he'd sent her home with little more than an appreciative thank-you.

He'd managed a couple hours of sleep before having to get the kids off to school and come to work. It was going to be difficult to focus on his classes today; his thoughts and prayers were all with his brother. A light tap on his open door drew his attention. Carl Young was standing there, a sympathetic expression on his dark face. He must have heard the news.

"Hey, Matt. I'm sorry about your brother. Have you heard anything?"

"Some. I talked to my mom a few minutes ago. He came through the first surgery all right, but there's another one yet to go." His brother had been shot three times and there'd been doubt in the beginning if he'd pull through. Praise God, he was holding his own so far.

"How are your parents holding up?"

"As well as can be expected."

"I'm praying for him."

"Thanks. Never can have too much of that."

"Amen."

"Who's running the store while your dad is gone?"

Matt leaned back in his chair, one hand on the armrest. "He hired an assistant manager earlier this year. Young guy named Troy Ballard."

"Good to hear. I was afraid you'd have to run the place for a while. Then that would leave me to take all your classes." Carl chuckled and winked.

One of the things Matt liked best about his friend was he could count on Carl to lighten any situation. "Get your ugly face out of here."

Carl waved and disappeared.

Shelby's arms pumped in rhythm with her stride as she kept pace with Pam on their daily walk. They'd had to postpone it to the afternoon due to a schedule change at Pam's job. The morning walks had quickly become something Shelby enjoyed. She was feeling stronger every day. Leading a healthy lifestyle was proving to be less of a torment than she'd expected.

"Are you serious?"

Shelby stopped suddenly, turning back to her friend, who stood still in the middle of the sidewalk, hands on hips.

Pam shook her head in disbelief. "I cannot believe your mother did such an underhanded thing to you. Deliberately giving Matt a phony address and phone number."

"Well, she did." Shelby waved her to catch up and resume their walk. She been telling her friend about the things that had been discovered when she and Matt had compared notes at the picnic yesterday. "I guess she thought she was doing me a favor."

"Some favor. Shel, your life could have been totally different."

"Maybe. But I do love my job, and Matt had a wonderful wife and two amazing kids. It all turned out the way it was supposed to, I guess."

"What now? I mean, do you and Matt have a future? Do you want one? Does he?"

The women walked in place at the street corner while they waited for a car to pass. "I doubt it. We're friends again. But as for anything more—well, he's been through the devastating loss of his wife to cancer. He's not going to get involved with someone who's going to be battling health issues all her life."

"It's not like you're dying or anything, Shel. Your heart condition is very minor. Easily managed with meds and taking good care of yourself."

"I don't think he sees it that way. He sees a woman who might die suddenly and leave him and his children grieving a second time."

"I guess I get it. To a point. Have you heard any more about his brother, Ty? I was just sick to hear about that. So horrible."

"Matt texted me earlier and said Ty came through the first surgery all right but he still has a long way to go." She sent up another prayer for Matt's brother.

They walked in silence for a while before Pam spoke again. "So. Do you love Matt?"

The question brought Shelby to a stop. "What are

you talking about?" Pam kept walking, forcing her to catch up.

"You have that same look on your face as you did that summer. You have the same tone of voice when you say his name. Your eyes get all dreamy when you talk about him or his kids. It's a perfectly logical question."

But there was no logical answer. The wall between them now was more like a small curb, easily crossed. The attraction was there on both sides, but as for anything more… "I don't know how to answer that."

"It's simple. Yes or no."

"Yes. I think I always have. I just didn't realize it until I came home and saw him again." He was the reason she'd never found someone to share her life. No one else had measured up.

"Then what are you going to do about it?"

"Nothing. Nothing at all."

Shelby pulled the mail from Matt's box as the school bus rolled to a stop in front of the house. She smiled and waved as Cassidy strolled up the driveway, receiving a halfhearted wave in return. She studied the child closely as she meandered to the sidewalk and plodded up the porch steps. "You all right?"

She shrugged, dropping her backpack on the floor. "I guess."

Resting a hand on the girl's shoulder, Shelby steered her to one of the wicker chairs. "What's wrong, sweetie?"

Cassidy remained silent a long moment, head bowed and shoulders slumped. "I hate the way I look."

Shelby inhaled slowly, her heart aching. She had to resist her impulse to pull Cassidy into her arms and tell her how beautiful she was. Her instincts told her that wasn't what the little girl needed to hear right now. "What don't you like?"

"Everything. My hair is boring and my face is yucky."

"How would you like to look?"

"Like my friend Molly. She wears cool makeup and stuff."

Shelby fought the urge to smile. Was there a female on the planet who hadn't felt the same way at one point in their lives? "Do you wear makeup?"

"No." She huffed, crossing her arms over her chest. "Dad won't let me. He says I'm too young."

Shelby took her small hand in hers. "Maybe if you told your dad how important this is to you, he'd change his mind."

"He won't. He wants to keep me a baby. I'm almost twelve. Besides, even if I could, I don't have anyone to show me how to put it on."

"I can show you." Shelby regretted the words the moment they left her mouth. She shouldn't be going against Matt's wishes.

"Would you?" Cassidy sprang to her feet, her face aglow. "That would be so cool."

Half an hour later, Cassidy and Shelby looked in the mirror of Shelby's bathroom at the final result of the makeover. Cassidy looked years older. Maybe too old. A niggling doubt crept into Shelby's mind. Cassidy was a pretty little girl. She had a fresh, natural beauty of her own. Looking at her now, Shelby wished she hadn't suggested this experiment. "You know, Cassidy, this has been fun, but it's too much makeup for you to wear to school. You know that, don't you?"

"No." Cassidy met her gaze with a pleading look. "It

looks good. I look like a teenager." She struck a pose, tilting her head at a coquettish angle.

Sadness settled around Shelby's heart. Cassidy was rushing toward something she wasn't ready for. "Let's wipe this off now."

"But it looks good." She leaned closer to the mirror, staring at her image.

Shelby dampened a rag and handed it to her. "Cassidy, you're a pretty girl. You don't need all this makeup."

A pout pulled down the corners of her mouth. "But I want to look like the girls in your magazine."

For the first time, Shelby experienced a rush of resentment toward the young women featured on *Tween Scene's* covers. "Cassidy, remember when I changed your picture to make you look like a cover model?"

"That was so awesome."

Shelby gently took the girl's face between her hands. "The girls on the covers look exactly like you. We change all the pictures that way. Wait. I'll show you." Shelby moved into her room and retrieved a candid photo from her briefcase.

"Who's that?" Cassidy asked, studying the picture.

"Yasmine."

The girls eyes widened. "No way. I saw the cover of your magazine. She was perfect."

Shelby nodded. "That's what she really looks like before the makeup and hairstylist and the special lighting. And of course the computer enhancements." Shelby watched as the child digested this new information and her shoulders slumped.

"She looks like a regular old girl," Cassidy lamented.

Shelby gently took the little girl's hands in her own. "We all look like regular girls, sweetheart."

Cassidy frowned. "But I want to look beautiful."

"I know. All women do, and makeup helps us look our best, but we have to be careful not to use too much."

Cassidy looked in the mirror at her freshly scrubbed face and frowned. "Now I look like dumb old me."

Shelby rested her hands on the girl's shoulders, peering at their reflections. "Smile for me." Cassidy pouted for a moment then complied. "When you smile, it's like the sun coming out. You have a smile like your daddy's."

Cassidy giggled. "He says I have my mommy's smile."

Shelby ignored the sting in her heart. This could have been her daughter. "Maybe what you really need is a new look. Next time we'll play with your hair and try some new styles. Sometimes a new haircut can change your whole attitude."

"Cool. Thanks, Shelby." Cassidy twisted around and gave her a hug. "You're the best. I'm so glad you moved here. Hey, could I invite some of my friends over and you could show us how to do makeup and hair? For regular girls like us, I mean."

"Sure. I think that's a great idea."

Cassidy's face lit up. "I have a better idea."

Shelby gave her a wary look. "What?"

"We could do it at my slumber party. We could stay up all night doing hair and makeup and order pizza and stuff."

Shelby liked the idea. She'd enjoy doing girl things with Cassidy, but she'd also welcome an opportunity to teach her and her friends the truth and dispel some misconceptions. "I'd love to help out. You need to okay this with your dad though, and it might be a good idea to check with your friends' mothers. Make sure they know what we're going to do because some moms may not want them trying out makeup yet."

"Cool."

"When is your party?"

"This Friday." Cassidy turned away quickly, walking out into the bedroom.

"Oh?" Odd. Matt hadn't mentioned it to her and he usually kept her apprised of all the children's activities for the week. But then, the party was on Friday and he was off that day, so he probably didn't see any reason to tell her since she wouldn't be involved. Hopefully he wouldn't object to her putting in an appearance at the party.

Matt closed the dishwasher and started the cycle. Kenny was tucked in bed and Cassidy should be on her way. As if sensing his thoughts, she appeared at his side, an impish grin on her face. That usually spelled trouble. He eyed her skeptically. "What?"

"I love you, Daddy."

He grimaced, tossing the dishtowel over his shoulder. "Yeah, yeah. Out with it."

"Can I have a slumber party this Friday night? Please? Please?"

Matt sighed in mild irritation. "Sweetheart, we've had this discussion before."

Cassidy set her fists on her hips and frowned. "I know. We have to have another grown-up in the house. But I don't see why."

He hated to deny his daughter a party, but she didn't understand. He looked at Cassidy's disappointed expression and felt himself weakening. "I don't know, kiddo."

Cassidy pounced on the crack in his defenses. "I know. I'll bet Miss Shelby would do it."

"Do what?"

"Chaperone." She smiled gleefully. "We were going to do the makeup thing anyway. I know she'd do it. She's here all the time now anyhow."

He was all too aware of that fact. "What makeup thing?"

Cassidy waved off his question. "It's girl stuff, Dad. You wouldn't get it."

"Why don't we wait until your Gramma gets back from Dallas and she can come stay with us that night."

Cassidy assumed her drooping noodle position. Shoulders sagging, head leaned back, knees bent. It was a pitiful sight. He waited for the whine that always followed.

"No. She won't be back until Sunday. I want someone cool like Shelby to do it."

"Cassidy."

She straightened and tried again. "Please? Can I at least ask her?"

Matt inhaled deeply. "Let me think about it."

It was later that night before Matt could consider how to handle Cassidy's request. He didn't want to refuse his daughter yet again, but asking Shelby to take on such a huge responsibility went beyond the duties they'd agreed to. Besides, this Friday was his day off. He couldn't ask her to work overtime. He was sure she would welcome the break. He thought about his daughter's excitement. He had to at least try. Didn't he?

He picked up the phone and dialed, a smile coming unbidden to his lips when she answered. "Can you meet me outside for a second? I need to talk to you." He hung up, not exactly sure why he'd turned a phone call into a face-to-face other than he wanted to see her again.

She came toward him across the driveway, her hair

shimmering in the light from the streetlamps. She smiled into his eyes, and he forgot to breathe.

"Hey. What's going on? It sounded serious."

The sight of her jumbled his thinking and he had to regroup. "Did Cassidy say anything to you about a party this week?"

"You mean her slumber party? Yes. She's really excited."

Matt exhaled a huff of irritation. Apparently his daughter was trying to pull an end run on him. "I haven't given my permission yet."

"Oh. I didn't know. She acted as if it was all settled."

Her calm response confirmed his daughter's scheme. "That's what I was afraid of."

"What's this about?"

Matt rubbed his forehead. "She's been after me for some time to have a slumber party and I keep making excuses. I don't know how to explain to her that a single dad having a bunch of little girls overnight…"

"Oh. I see your problem."

"I don't know what to say to her, and I can't keep making up excuses. Lately when I tell her no she flies into a fit of tears for no reason or turns into a drama queen. She never used to do that. It's like she's an alien creature."

Shelby laughed lightly. "Girls aren't that much of a mystery, Matt. We want to be loved. We want to be taken seriously and respected. We want the men in our lives to listen to us but not always fix everything. But mostly, we want to be cherished and protected."

Matt looked into Shelby's warm brown eyes. Cherished and protected. That's all he'd ever wanted to do for Shelby. But he couldn't protect her from a heart attack and that scared him. He sighed and shook his head. "You make it sound so simple."

"It is. So, are you going to let her have the slumber party?"

"If Mom or Laura were here, maybe. But as it is…"

"What if I acted as chaperone?"

"That was her idea, too." His eyes narrowed. "You sure you didn't cook this up together?"

"Scout's honor. But I certainly wouldn't mind. Now, before you say no, let me explain my idea. You and Kenny could hang around until nine or so then go to your mom's for the night. I'll stay with the girls. In the morning, you can come back and bring breakfast."

Her offer should have surprised him, but it didn't. He was all too aware of how much she cared for his son and daughter. It was part of his ongoing emotional struggle. He liked seeing her with his children. Too much. "I guess that would work. But are you sure you want to spend all night with a bunch of screaming pre-teen girls?"

Shelby chuckled softly. "I think I can manage Cassidy and a few of her friends. No more than six though."

He couldn't believe he was considering her suggestion. No matter how he looked at her idea, he couldn't find any fault in it. It would satisfy Cassidy's desire to have a party and keep him out of the picture when necessary. "I don't know. I really miss Katie at times like this."

Silence filled the space between them. He realized he'd said that last out loud.

"Matt, I'd be more than happy to chaperone her party if it's all right with you."

"Okay then. I'll let her know. And thanks, Shelby. You seem to be there whenever I need you."

A small smirk moved one corner of her lips. "That's me. Miss Dependable."

Matt watched her walk back inside her house, not missing the little dig she'd sent his way. He'd said she wasn't dependable, but she'd been there for him every time he had needed her. The one time she hadn't been wasn't her fault completely.

Slowly he turned and walked to the house. A few weeks ago he would never have allowed Shelby to get so close to his kids. Now she was playing mom, chaperoning a slumber party and weaving herself deeper and deeper into their lives.

The old fear in his gut was still there. Not that she'd suddenly run away, but what would happen when she eventually returned to New York? Sooner or later she would. He'd reminded the kids frequently that Shelby would be leaving at some point. So much so that they had started rolling their eyes in disgust. They'd cleared up the past, but it had only increased his longing for companionship. He was becoming more and more aware of the empty places in his heart and his life. Places he was beginning to think only Shelby could fill. But was he willing to risk everything on a woman who was ill?

Shelby pulled the large envelope from her Gramma's mailbox. The latest issue of *Tween Scene*. Her heart contracted when she remembered that this might be the last issue published. Taking a seat on the swing, she idly flipped through the pages, an uneasiness swelling in her mind. The images she used to consider hip and edgy now struck her as a bit exploitive. She kept comparing each too-thin model to Cassidy.

Her gaze drifted across the driveway to Matt's house. All her experience with preteens had been with models, pop stars and child actors. She'd never dealt with a real, normal young girl before. Someone like Cassidy. She thought about the online magazine she'd considered. It wouldn't be hard to do. She had the skills and the experience. Her mind began to fill with ideas. It might be fun. It would be wonderful to have control of the content and not have to compromise her convictions for the sake of sales.

Shelby hurried into the house, grabbed a pen and paper and a piece of fruit and went back to the front porch. Oh, how she missed her laptop. The first chance she got she would buy a new one. She was still scribbling ideas when the bus pulled up and Kenny bounded off. She watched with joy as he raced up the driveway toward her, all thoughts of the new magazine vanishing. What she wouldn't give to experience this feeling every day for the rest of her life.

"I won!" Kenny shouted, grabbing hold of Shelby's arm.

"What did you win?" Shelby asked, smiling. The little boy was bubbling over with excitement.

"I won the drawing contest at school." He dug into his backpack.

"That's wonderful. Congratulations."

"My picture of the woods was better than anybody else's. See what I won? This big thing of drawing paper and special drawing pens and a case and some colored pencils."

Shelby relieved him of the cumbersome assortment of prizes. "I'm so proud of you. Your daddy will be so happy." Kenny smiled and readily accepted the hug she offered. The feel of his sweet little body in her arms brought a lump to her throat.

"They're going to hang my picture in the front hall at school so everyone can see it."

"That's wonderful, Kenny. We'll all come and see it."

"Can we work on our scrapbook?" Kenny asked, stuffing his prizes back into his backpack.

"I think we'd better wait for Cassidy, don't you? She should be home as soon as her club meeting is over. Molly's mom is bringing her home."

"Okay," he agreed reluctantly.

"Why don't we have a quick snack and then take a walk on the trails? By the time we get back she should be almost home and we can work on the scrapbook."

"But she'll have homework to do."

"Well, maybe she won't have very much today." She took his hand and walked across the drive to his house.

The scrapbooking project Cassidy and Kenny had started was progressing nicely. They worked on it each day. Shelby's heart had been touched multiple times by the memories they shared. The fact that the scrapbook was a surprise gift for Matt only added to their joy. They'd collected a large variety of pictures, trinkets and other memorabilia to include in the book.

They worked diligently each afternoon, talking about happy times with their mother and sometimes shedding a few tears. Since they were determined to keep it a secret from Matt, watching the clock had become Shelby's main responsibility. Everything had to be put away and hidden before he came home. One day he'd come home early and nearly caught them. They'd been extra cautious from then on.

Every day she questioned her wisdom in agreeing to watch Matt's children. She was much too comfortable in his home, and she cared too deeply for his children. Her time with them was like experiencing a tantalizing dream beyond her reach. No matter how hard she tried, or prayed, it would never come true.

Their relationship had vastly improved since their talk at the picnic. Things were more relaxed and comfortable. Much of their old camaraderie had returned. They talked or texted frequently during the day, mostly about the kids or Ty's ongoing recovery. But sometimes Matt would call for no apparent reason. A few times he'd called to ask her a question or remind her about an appointment one of the children had.

Lately, he'd been calling even more. And when he got home, he had been asking for more and more details about the children's day. She had the impression he wanted someone to talk to, and she was more than happy to oblige, even though it was a bittersweet experience. She didn't want to be his sounding board for a few weeks; she wanted to be in his life forever.

She had to constantly remind herself that rekindling an old friendship wasn't the same as rekindling an old love. But Lord forgive her, she counted the moments until she heard his voice.

Matt pulled into his driveway, coming to a stop near the back door. The lights were on in the house, but he was pretty sure Shelby would be asleep. He had to call upon her generosity as babysitter once again. He'd agreed to fill in for his mother at an important campaign event this evening in her absence. Not his cup of tea, but with her still in Dallas with Ty, he was happy to step in.

He climbed out of the car, glancing again at the faint light in the window. He liked knowing there was someone waiting for him. That Shelby was waiting for him.

Somewhere along the way he'd started looking forward to talking to her and hearing her voice. He looked forward to coming home each night and finding her there, helping Cassidy with supper or playing a game with Kenny. The sight of her and his children as he came through the door filled him with a happiness he'd long forgotten. His kids were happy. They adored Shelby. He was grateful to her for that. There was huge comfort in knowing someone else loved them as much as he did. And Shelby did love the kids. It was obvious.

How did she feel about him?

The attraction between them was still there, rekindled no doubt by the closeness required by her baby-sitting duties. Shelby was a beautiful woman. With her big brown eyes and her deceptively delicate appearance, any normal male would be drawn to her. He was more vulnerable than most, that's all. And, while he no longer feared Shelby would break his children's hearts, he wasn't ready to risk his own.

Matt entered through the back door as quietly as possible. It was after midnight. He'd been cornered with questions about his brother as well as his mother's position on several local issues, but he hadn't expected to be this late. He wouldn't blame her if she was upset. She'd agreed to babysit for a few hours each day, not around the clock. The big house was silent. Too silent.

Frowning he walked through the hall into the living room. The television screen was blue and silent. The small lights on the DVD player and the home theater equipment were on. Odd. Why hadn't Shelby turned it off? And where was she?

He shut off the electronics, then turned around. He froze. Shelby was sound asleep on the sofa, the afghan pulled up near her chin. He opened his mouth to call her name but stopped, captivated by the appealing picture she made. Her dark hair was mussed. Featherlight tendrils fell in wisps across her cheek. One hand lay against her face; bright pink nail polish contrasted against the dark tresses.

His heart ached. They'd had so many dreams, so many plans. But too many things had conspired against them back then. Shelby looked so peaceful. So beautiful. He leaned over, his fingers brushing soft curls from her cheek.

She moaned.

Matt straightened and quickly left the room. In the kitchen he rested his hands against the counter, battling the emotions that were swirled deep inside. Everything he'd ever wanted, every dream he'd had, was lying asleep on his sofa. The first woman he'd ever loved was only a few feet away. And years removed.

Guilt pierced his conscience. Katie had been all he'd ever hoped for. He'd loved her with his whole heart, but she was so different from Shelby that he wondered if he'd deliberately looked for someone as opposite as he could find. Someone who could never remind him of the woman he'd lost.

Seeing her tonight, so vulnerable, made him realize what a slippery slope he was on. He was falling in love with her again, and he couldn't afford to. They could never pick up where they left off. It was too late and there was too much at stake. But he didn't want to be alone anymore.

Katie was still in his heart, but her memory now left a sweetness behind, not the knife-edge of grief it once was. Maybe it was time to move on.

Right now he had to send Shelby home. Fantasizing was a waste of time. He started back into the living room, stubbing his toe against the Bombay chest.

"Matt? Is that you?"

The sleepy voice sent his blood tingling. He swallowed the lump in his throat. "Yeah. It's me."

Shelby sat up and smiled. Matt's heart jumped into his throat. She was the most beautiful woman he'd ever seen. All he wanted at this moment was to take her into his arms and kiss her the way he'd longed to under the oak tree at the picnic.

"How did it go?" She squinted at him from behind drowsy eyelids.

"Good. Sorry I'm so late."

"Don't worry about it." She shook her head. "We had a nice evening. I dug out an old movie and made some popcorn. It's been very relaxing."

She smiled, a silly, sleepy grin, and every bone in his body turned to liquid. "Good. That's good."

"Well. I'd better go." She stood and started to fold the afghan. "The kids' homework is on the table ready for you to sign. I checked it over. There's a permission slip for Kenny's field trip and a notice about tryouts for chorus for Cassidy. Oh, and you might want to remind your mom that next Tuesday is Grandparents' Day at the school."

She laid the afghan across the back of the couch, then turned and faced him. "Something wrong?"

He knew he could never adequately answer that question. Yes. Everything was wrong. He was in falling in love with her, and he was afraid it was too late to stop it.

"No. Just tired."

"Then I'd better get out of here so you can get some rest. Oh, and remember, tomorrow is the big slumber party."

"Right." He nodded, following her to the door, keeping a safe distance. If he got too close, if he felt the warmth of her, smelled the sweet scent of her, he might do something he'd regret. He reached for the doorknob. Shelby abruptly turned, bringing her up against his chest. His face was only inches from her. He stared at her lips.

"Oh, I'm so sorry. I, uh, forgot my cell phone."

Matt looked down into her brown eyes and forgot to breathe. The warmth of her beneath his hands, her fragrance, set his heart pounding. He'd known if he ever got this close he'd be unable to resist taking her into his arms.

The air in the room stilled, awareness arced between them. His brain told him to let go. Step away. Put some space between them before he gave into his desire to kiss her. He gripped her shoulders and set her away from him. Quickly, he turned and retrieved her cell from the end table. When he stood in front of her again, she was staring at the floor, fidgeting.

She looked up and smiled, reaching for the phone, her fingers wrapping around his own. He saw her lips part. Slowly he released the phone, only to find his hands grasping her shoulders again and pulling her closer.

He knew he should stop, but the attraction between them was a force bigger than he could resist. His hand lightly cupped her cheek. She sighed, resting her head against his palm. Her movement was his undoing. He slid his hand along her neck, pulling her toward him. He couldn't take his eyes off her mouth. He lowered his head, heart pounding in anticipation.

He inhaled her breath, then carefully touched his lips to hers. Her mouth was warm, pliant. He remembered the sweet taste of her and the perfect way she fit against him. She clung to him, returning his kiss. He was sinking in the wonder of her, drowning. He had to surface or be lost forever.

He released her but was unable to take his eyes from hers. He'd known from the moment he'd first seen her he'd lose his heart again. It was why he'd fought so hard. If she'd stayed away, he could have kept his love buried. But now here he was. Lost.

He'd been lonely but comfortable in his grief. Shelby had come home and forced him out of his apathy, forced him to come alive again and confront part of his grief he'd buried. But she'd also brought with her a risk. The risk of losing her, of facing the possibility of loss again. He wasn't strong enough, his kids shouldn't have to face that again.

"Shelly, why did you come back?" It was barely a whisper. He wasn't sure if he'd said the words aloud or not.

Shelby inhaled sharply and stepped back. Without a word, she turned and walked out, the thud of the door the only sound in the empty room.

Chapter Eleven

Shelly. He'd called her Shelly. His pet name for her. Shelby pressed her fingers to her lips, fighting back the tears. The kiss had sealed her fate. She was hopelessly, forever in love with Matt. She should never have let that happen.

But she'd wanted him to kiss her. She'd wanted it so badly. She'd been playing house for weeks, imagining herself as part of his life. Tonight the dream had come true, his kiss had been the fulfillment of all her desires. Then he had shattered the dream with a few words. *Why did you come back?*

Shelby curled up in the chair in her room, staring out the window. What had he meant? You're ruining my life? You're digging up pain? Probably all of that. He'd made it clear all along how he felt. She shouldn't read too much into a kiss, one weak moment on both their parts. To be honest, the attraction was still there, but that's all it was. Attraction alone wasn't enough to build a life on.

She closed her eyes, reliving the kiss once again. Matt cared about her, but did he care enough to accept her as is, flaws and all? A knife-edge of sadness twisted in her heart. Doubtful. And she couldn't blame him. He and the kids had lost so much. How could she expect them to willingly walk into that valley again? Her situation wasn't anything like cancer, but living with the uncertainty, the threat of something happening, would be like walking the edge of a cliff every day. No one could live like that.

Tears stung her eyes and she lifted her gaze upward. "Father, You know how much I love those children." The Lord might never have intended for her to have a life with Matt and his children, but He'd shown her what her future could be. He'd restored her faith and redirected her life. To ask for anything more would be greedy.

The ache in her heart squeezed tighter, choking off her air. She drew her knees up to her chin and gave in to the tears. Her mind might rationalize the pain away, but her heart grieved.

"The number you are calling is unavailable." Matt listened to the monotone voice in his ear, then tossed his cell phone onto the counter. He stared out the kitchen window at Shelby's house and the empty driveway. Where was she? It was Friday. The day of the slumber party. He'd realized he had no idea what to expect or how to prepare. He needed to talk to Shelby, but her car had been gone since early morning and she wasn't answering her cell. He'd tried to reach her all day between Handy Works projects, but she'd not returned his calls.

He pinched the bridge of his nose. He wasn't looking forward to seeing her after last night. He didn't know whether to apologize for kissing her or behave as if nothing had happened. All he knew for certain was that last night had changed everything. He loved her and he could no longer deny it. If her response to the kiss was any indication, she had feelings for him, as well.

So what? It didn't change a thing. All it proved was they were both attracted. That alone didn't spell a future together.

Swallowing his pride, Matt picked up the phone and dialed Shelby's cell again. No answer. Where had she been all day? Had she forgotten her phone? He checked his watch. It was nearing time for Cassidy to get home from school, and she'd have questions and he had no answers.

An hour later he called Shelby's cell again. It went directly to voice mail. A grain of apprehension formed in his gut. If he couldn't locate Shelby in time, he'd have to find a backup chaperone for tonight. His parents weren't due home until Sunday. That left Laura. She was coming home for the weekend.

He paced the kitchen impatiently as he waited for his sister to answer. "You have any idea where Shelby might be?"

"Uh, no. I'm out of town all week. Why would I know that?"

"You two talk don't you?"

"Yes, but only briefly and she doesn't give me her hourly schedule. Why? What's up?"

Matt explained. "I don't understand why she doesn't answer."

"Could be any number of reasons. Don't worry about it. I'm sure she'll show up. She wouldn't miss this slumber party. She's as excited as Cassidy."

"I suppose you're right." He sighed, refusing to think the worst. His sister was right about one thing. Shelby would never disappoint Cassidy.

He called Shelby's phone several more times but she

didn't answer. A knot of anger and anxiety began to form in his gut. No. She wouldn't. She wouldn't leave without saying goodbye. He had to stop thinking the worst.

His cell rang and Laura's name appeared.

"Is she there yet?"

Matt clenched his jaw, trying to quell the knot growing in his gut. "No."

Laura sighed into the phone. "I don't understand. Why doesn't she answer?"

He could find only one explanation for her to be out of touch this long. She was gone and avoiding his calls. He didn't want to believe that, but what other reason could there be?

"No." Laura's voice broke into his dour thoughts. "I know what you're thinking, but you're wrong. Don't jump to conclusions."

"I should have seen this coming."

Laura growled into the phone, "Mathias Durrant, I'd like to wring your neck. There's a perfectly good explanation, and you'll feel like a worm when you hear what it is."

He wanted to believe that. "You're probably right."

"I know I am. In fact, I'll bet she shows up before Cassidy gets off the bus. Have a little faith."

His faith waned, and fear and anger rose as time passed and Shelby failed to appear. He prayed his sister was right, but an hour later when Shelby was still not home, Matt had to face the truth. She'd done it again. She'd grown tired of the small-town life and run back to her career. Only this time, it wasn't his heart she'd left broken in pieces, but his children's.

Matt stood on the front porch waiting with a sick dread in the pit of his stomach. Cassidy had been bouncing off the walls all week with excitement over her slumber party. Now he had to tell her it wasn't going to happen? He watched as his daughter darted off the school bus, her expression filled with joy and excitement. Matt's heart ached. She would be devastated. Not only would she not have her slumber party, but Shelby's departure would crush her.

His cell rang again. Laura. "She's not home."

"Oh, Matt."

He turned away from the sight of his child skipping up the driveway toward him. "How am I going to tell her?"

"Don't. Not yet. The party doesn't start for hours yet. I'll be home around then. I'll fill in if you need me to."

Matt exhaled a tense breath. "She needs to be prepared for the worst."

"*She* does, or *you* do?"

Laura's question was like a thorn in his spirit that he tried to ignore. This wasn't about him.

Matt gave Shelby another half hour before taking his daughter aside. "Cassidy, I think we need to talk." He pulled her onto the sofa beside him, searching frantically for the right words. "We may have to cancel your slumber party."

Dark blue eyes widened with surprise. "Why? What did I do?"

The tremor in her voice broke his heart. "Nothing. It's not you, sweetie. It's Shelby. I think she's gone back home. To New York."

Tears welled up in her eyes, trickling quickly down her cheeks. "No. She wouldn't go without saying goodbye. Besides, she's going to be our chaperone. I've told everyone about her. We're going to do magazine makeup, and she's going to do pictures of my friends like she did me and…" A sob erupted from her throat. She rested her head on his shoulder. "No. She wouldn't do that."

Matt held her close, wishing he could cry himself. He'd believed in Shelby, too. Look what it got him. "She was gone when I got up this morning. She probably missed the big city and decided to go back home."

"You're wrong." Cassidy pushed him away. "You don't like her. I thought you did. You said you were friends, but you're always telling us she'll go away. You're glad she's gone."

Was he glad? There had been a time when he could have answered honestly yes. Now, all he felt was aching sadness and the sting of betrayal again. Right now, what mattered was his daughter's tender heart.

"Everything will be all right. I'll be the chaperone tonight—"

"I don't want you here," Cassidy wailed, sobbing again. "You're a boy! This is a girl night!"

Matt held up his hand. "Only until your aunt Laura gets here. She's on her way home, and she said she'll come and stay so you can have your party."

"That's not the same. I want Miss Shelby. I love her."

Kenny and Chester darted through the room. "Hey. Miss Shelby is home. Can I go see her?"

Cassidy ran to the window, then turned and dashed for the door. "Daddy! She's here. I told you she hadn't left."

Matt walked out onto the front porch. Cassidy ran up to Shelby as she got out of her car and gave her a hug. Matt knew she was spilling her guts and he cringed at the same moment his cell rang again. "She's here."

Laura grunted in his ear. "Imagine that. She showed up in time."

Her sarcasm hit its mark. "Cutting it kind of close."

His sister's tone was icy when she spoke. "If you don't wake up and take that log out of your eye, you're going to lose something special. Is that what you really want?"

Matt watched from the porch as Shelby and Cassidy walked toward him. Shelby looked angry. He braced for the confrontation.

"See, Dad. I told you she hadn't left."

Shelby raised her chin, her brown eyes shooting sparks. "I had a doctor's appointment in Jackson. And then I had some shopping to do. I didn't realize I was supposed to report my comings and goings to you."

"I've been calling you since nine this morning. You couldn't have been at the doctor's all this time." Inwardly, he cringed at his accusatory tone. He shouldn't be attacking her. He should be telling her how relieved and how grateful he was that she hadn't broken Cassidy's heart.

"I turned off my phone and forgot to turn it back on. It happens."

"What was I supposed to think?" She could have at least called and explained her absence.

"That I wouldn't let Cassidy down." She pushed past him and walked into the house with his daughter.

Matt ran a hand through his hair. Why were they always at odds? No. *They* weren't. *He* was. He thought he'd gotten past his fear that Shelby would run off again. She'd proven her reliability over and over since she'd been watching the children. But a part of him was still wary. Laura had warned him he might be losing something special. He knew she was right, but how did he let go and trust Shelby again? How did he let himself love a woman who was sick?

* * *

"Molly and Darcy are here!" Cassidy squealed, dashing to the front door.

Shelby gathered her courage. The slumber party had officially begun. Matt had made himself scarce since she'd arrived, for which she was grateful. His sour attitude would have dampened her excitement, not to mention Cassidy's.

Matt's lack of faith hurt. She'd thought they'd gotten beyond the old issues, but she was beginning to think Matt would never completely trust her, or anyone, with his heart ever again. His depth of mistrust and fear of loss could never be overcome. Her main goal now was to make sure Cassidy had the best slumber party possible. Matt would have to deal with his resentment in his own way.

Everything was ready. Food. Movies. Games. She'd bought a new laptop that afternoon, complete with the software she needed for image enhancement. Cassidy was eager to share her new discovery with her friends. It was going to be the highlight of the evening.

Several hours later, Shelby curled up in the chair in Matt's downstairs guest room. It was near enough to the living room to hear the girls if they called, yet private enough that she could get some sleep if possible. Not that she planned on getting much sleep. The girls were giggling and laughing. The music was loud. That meant the evening was a success.

She'd taught the girls all about makeup. They'd taken pictures and tweaked them the way she'd done for Cassidy, only this time it came with a discussion of what was real and what was fake, what was appropriate and what wasn't. She'd been surprised at the girls' wisdom. One girl had brought up the fact that the Lord expected them to behave and dress one way and the world another. It was a topic that went on for some time since a few of the girls apparently didn't attend church.

Their discussion had convinced her that starting a Christian magazine for young girls was a good idea. She had a new desire to publish what was inspiring and supportive, instead of encouraging them to dress and act like celebrities. It wasn't that *Tween Scene* did anything wrong, but she wanted to create something better. Reaching for her drink, she realized the house had gone silent. Not a good thing at a slumber party.

She peeked around the corner at the living room. Sleeping bags filled with little girls covered the floor. Tousled hair peeked out of the covers and little feet protruded from blankets.

Every flat surface in the room was covered with food or makeup. She smiled. She couldn't remember the last time she'd had so much fun, when she'd known such joy and a sense of belonging. Teaching Cassidy's friends about makeup had kept them all in stitches. They'd giggled and laughed until tears rolled down their cheeks.

"Thank you, Father, for this opportunity." She would cherish these memories forever.

A blanket moved, causing Chester to raise his head from his comfy spot beside his mistress. Cassidy sat up and smiled, her eyes drowsy but bright with happiness. Shelby waved.

The girl scooted out from under the covers and hurried toward her, throwing her arms around her neck. "Thank you. Thank you, Miss Shelby. This is the best party ever. I'll love you forever." She kissed Shelby's cheek, then scurried back to bed.

The lump in her throat made it hard to swallow. Fighting tears, she turned and walked back to the guest room and crawled into bed. This is what she wanted. This is what her life should be about. A home. A family. Children.

She loved Matt. She loved his children. She would gladly spend the rest of her life raising them, but the wounds she'd inflicted ran too deep for him to overcome. Her health issues were an obstacle that Matt shouldn't have to confront ever again. She couldn't go on pretending, living a life that could never be hers. It wasn't fair to Matt and his children, and it wasn't fair to her.

Her leave was almost up. Gramma would be home in a few days. Maybe it was time for her to return to New York. Go back to the life she knew and let Matt return to his.

The realization sent a lance of sadness through her heart.

Matt and Kenny stepped through the front door Saturday morning and stopped in their tracks. The room resembled a bedding store after an earthquake. He looked closer and saw little heads sticking out here and there. No one stirred.

He glanced down at his son, putting his finger to his lips, indicating silence. "Come on, kiddo. Let's go around to the back door so we don't wake anyone." Shelby was perched on a stool at the counter, sipping coffee when they entered. "Good morning."

Her smile was welcoming, though a bit droopy. He doubted if she'd gotten much sleep. "We brought sustenance." He held up a box of fresh doughnuts. "How did it go?"

"Chester." Kenny reached down to hug his dog, who came trotting over. "Can I have a doughnut now?"

Matt nodded and filled a cup with fresh coffee. "Any problems?"

"Not a one. They were perfect little angels. Even Chester behaved. The girls all loved him."

He grinned. It felt natural to have Shelby waiting for him this morning. "Looks like they left a perfect little mess in there."

She shoved the doughnut carton to the far side of the counter. "The bigger the mess, the better the party."

"I'll remember that for next time."

Shelby glanced downward, staring into her cup. Was she thinking the same as he? Next time would happen without her participation.

"How about you bachelors?" She extended her arm, drawing Kenny to her side.

"We lived wild and free, didn't we, sport?" Matt ruffled his son's hair.

"We got pizza at bedtime," Kenny proclaimed. "It was awesome."

The doorbell chimed and shuffling noises commenced in the living room.

"That's probably Anna's mom. She said she'd have to pick her up early this morning." Shelby rose and moved to the other room.

Matt followed behind, wondering at the ease with which she'd assumed command of his household. Cassidy met him in the hall.

"Good morning, Daddy." She smiled and wrapped her arms around his waist.

He kissed the top of her head. "Good morning, sweetheart. Did you have fun?"

She nodded. "It was the best ever."

He hugged her again. It was all worth it. The worry. The doubt. The second-guessing about leaving Shelby in charge. His little girl was happy. Matt watched his daughter scurry back into the jumble of the living room. Shelby stood in the center of the room, smiling, laughing with the girls as they started to gather their belongings. She slipped an arm around Cassidy and pulled her close.

It was a simple gesture, but it left him breathless. He stared at the tableau before him, blinking as Kenny tore into the scene, skidding to a stop at Shelby's side and taking her hand.

The doorbell sounded again, breaking the spell.

Parents started to arrive in a steady stream to pick up their daughters. Matt pushed through the door with a sleeping bag and a satchel on his fourth trip to a car. Shelby was on the porch saying goodbye to one of the girls and her mother.

"Mrs. Durrant, I can't thank you enough for doing this. I wish I could let Addison have a slumber party, but I don't think I could stand the chaos. You're a brave mother."

Matt stopped cold. His started to correct the woman, but common courtesy told him to let it pass. His gaze locked with Shelby's, and he saw his own discomfort reflected in her soft brown eyes. Mrs. Durrant. His wife.

Shelby retreated into the house. He deposited the last guest's belongings in their car and waved goodbye. Slowly he started back inside. Cassidy and Shelby were wrapped in a bear hug when he entered the living room. "I love you. Thank you so much." Cassidy tilted her head back and gave Shelby a huge smile.

"You're welcome, sweetie. I had a great time, too."

Cassidy yawned and stepped back. "I'm going to bed. I'm sleepy."

Shelby watched her go, a tender smile on her face.

She turned to him and the smile vanished. His heart pounded. Realization hit him like a sledgehammer to his chest. She belonged here, with him, in his home as surely as he did. She started around the room, picking up glasses and half-empty snack bags. He moved toward her, taking her wrist in his hand as she reached for an empty bowl. "Leave all this. I'll do it later. You've done enough. More than enough, and I'm so grateful. Cassidy had a wonderful time."

"Me, too."

He held her wrist, pulling her around to face him. He looked into her eyes and saw her anxiety reflected back at him. Being back together had rekindled embers long damped. He wanted to hold her again, kiss her and never let her go. He was losing his battle, trying to keep her out of his heart. Trying to keep his own heart safe from loss. Touching her face, he said, "How can I ever thank you for what you've done?"

"No thanks are necessary. I love spending time with your children."

"What about their father? Do you like spending time with him?" He hadn't intended to ask that question, but now he found himself bracing for her answer.

"I always have."

She lowered her lashes, but not before he saw the love in her eyes. The same love that had burned so strongly fifteen years ago. Instead of filling him with joy it filled him with fear. This rekindled romance didn't have a happy ending. It couldn't.

She was so loving. So amazing. "Why haven't you ever married? You should have a family of your own." Sadness flashed through her eyes before she looked away.

"I never found anyone who— Anyone I wanted to spend my life with, I guess."

He reached out to her but she stepped away, a stiff smile on her face.

"I've got to go. I'm too old to have this much fun. I need a long nap, too." She slipped past him and walked to the door, closing it behind her. His house and his heart felt empty.

Fatigue and letdown from the slumber party hit Shelby the moment she entered Gramma's house. But after a long nap, a shower and a healthy meal, she was feeling human again.

Pouring another glass of tea, she set her new laptop on the kitchen table and waited for it to power up. She had to work on something. Otherwise her conflicting emotions would tie her in knots. How was she supposed to watch Matt's children and pretend that they hadn't shared that earthquake of a kiss? How could she go along acting as if they were friends when she wanted more? The answer was she couldn't.

In the shower, the water had released the fatigue and tension; it had also washed away her emotional cobwebs and showed her what she needed to do. It was time to go back to New York. Funny thing was, she didn't want to. There was nothing there to go back to but an empty apartment and probably the unemployment line. But she couldn't stay here either. She couldn't stay here in Dover and see Matt and the kids and not be part of their lives. She couldn't be content with being simply a neighbor and friend. She loved them too much. She wanted to be with them forever. But how did she get past the wall between her and Matt?

Gramma was due home in a few days. She'd spend the week with her, then go back up north on the weekend. It was the right thing to do. Shelby pressed her lips together to keep from crying. She opened her email and scanned the long list. One from her boss caught her breath. The decision about the future of Harmon Publishing would be announced at a special meeting Monday morning.

Waves of uncertainly and dread crashed into her mind. Quickly she read through the other emails, trying to find some hint of what was to come. Opinions among her colleagues ranged from minimum layoffs to a complete shutdown of the company. Either way, she, along with many others, were likely looking at unemployment.

Worrying about her health was scary enough. Worrying about her livelihood was paralyzing. Thankfully, she had savings and a few investments, but they were for her retirement, and she didn't want to tap those funds unless it was an emergency.

If she'd learned nothing else from this journey home, she'd learned to let go of things she couldn't control. But that meant keeping her mind on something else. Unfortunately, the something else was that kiss.

What she needed was something fun and creative to do. Like her plan for an online magazine. Ideas had been rolling around in her mind from the moment she'd awakened that afternoon and she couldn't wait to get them organized. Within a few hours she had a rough draft of her magazine all laid out.

The knock on the door was a unwelcome intrusion. "What now?" Growling under her breath, she went to the door, surprised to find Matt on the other side. The sight of him brought the kiss vividly to her mind, weakening her knees. She swallowed and tried to shove it aside. "Oh. Hey." He smiled, which started her memories replaying again.

"Do you have a minute? I'd like to talk to you."

She couldn't imagine why he was here. There wasn't anything to talk about. "Sure." She stepped back, allowing him to enter. "Let's go to the sunroom." She led the way, acutely aware of him behind her. They'd formed a comfortable friendship over the last weeks, but the kiss and his distrust had put them on shaky ground again.

Entering the sunroom, Shelby quickly wished she'd suggested the formal living room instead. This room was too small, too intimate. She motioned for him to sit and took a seat in her favorite chair in the corner, a safe distance from Matt.

She waited. Matt sat on edge of the chair, forearms resting on his thighs. She sensed his tension.

"Shelby, I wanted to thank you again for chaperoning the party. Cassidy hasn't stopped talking about it. She's on the phone now reliving every moment with her friends."

"I'm glad. But you thanked me this morning, Matt."

He nodded. "But I didn't apologize for doubting you. I should have known you'd never do that to Cassidy."

"Apparently not. But this isn't about me. It's about you. You'll never forgive me for leaving you, and I understand." Shelby stared at her hands. "I guess no matter what I do, you'll never trust me fully. So let me apologize to you. I'm sorry for breaking our engagement. I'm sorry I didn't wait and try to understand. I'm sorry I didn't try and contact you again. It just wasn't meant to be."

Matt shook his head. "When you didn't show, when I couldn't get in touch with you, it was like reliving that old hurt. Only this time it was going to hurt my daughter."

"I love that little girl." Tears sprang up in her eyes, and she quickly swiped them away.

Matt stood and came toward her, taking a seat on the ottoman beside the chaise. "I'm sorry. When it comes to my kids, I'm a bit—"

"Overprotective?"

"Now you sound like my dad."

Matt reached out and touched his fingers to the back of her hand. "There's something else I want to sort out." He looked into her eyes. "What happened between us the other night."

Shelby chewed her lip, fighting the mounting anxiety in her stomach. She was afraid to look at him. "There's nothing to sort out. We both got caught up in old feelings. Being together so much complicated things. It didn't mean anything."

"Is that how you really feel?"

She wanted to believe it was disappointment she heard in his voice, but she knew it was relief. He regretted kissing her and wanted to make sure it didn't happen again. "Why do you want to know?"

"I don't know. That's why I'm here, I guess. Having you back in my life, seeing you every day, made me remember what we once had."

"That was a long time ago. Besides, it doesn't matter. I'm going back to New York."

"You're leaving?"

"It's time."

"Just like that?" Matt stood and walked to the window, his hands resting on his hips.

"Not just like that. I'm pretty sure I'm going to be unemployed soon. I need to get back and start looking for another job." What would he do if she told him the real truth, that she loved him and she'd never stopped? What would he say if she explained how much she wanted to be part of his life? His children's lives? Nothing could change the fact that she had health issues. She couldn't guarantee something more serious wouldn't crop up. The risk would always there, hanging over her head, and she would never ask him to endure that with her.

There remained one more painful task. She had to tell the children she was going back home. In some ways that would be the more difficult task because three hearts would be broken, and she knew hers would never, ever heal.

"But what about my kids? They'll be upset. Heartbroken."

"I know. But I've tried to prepare them. I never told anyone I'd stay here permanently. And besides, there's no reason for me to stay. Is there?"

Matt blue eyes darkened. "No. None that I can think of."

Chapter Twelve

Shelby exited the side door in the Hope Chapel sanctuary and started toward the parking lot. She'd joined Pam and her family at church today. But with Matt and the children seated in her direct line of sight to the pulpit, she'd found it hard to concentrate on the sermon. The moment the benediction was finished, she quickly made her departure and headed for the door. She wanted to avoid Matt. Speaking to him would only shatter what was left of her broken heart. She unlocked her car, only to freeze in her tracks when she heard her name called.

"Miss Shelby."

Cassidy and Kenny ran up to her. Matt followed a short distance behind.

"Gramma and Grandpa are coming home from Dallas today. We're going to pick them up at the airport. You wanna come?"

Kenny nodded, taking Shelby's hand as if to pull her along with him. "Yeah, our uncle Ty is getting better, so they can come home now."

She'd like nothing better. If she had her way, she'd do everything with these precious children. "I'd like to, but I have something to take care of this afternoon. Say hello for me, though."

"Okay."

The children moved off and climbed into their SUV, which she realized was parked only a few spots away from her car. Matt stood in front of her. She forced herself to stay calm despite the knot of nerves in her stomach. "I'd like to take the kids for pizza later if that's all right with you."

Matt frowned. "Why?"

"I want to tell them I'm leaving. I thought it should come from me first."

He held her gaze a moment then nodded. "All right. We'll be back from Jackson around four. Call when you're ready to go."

Shelby watched him walk away. Ready to go? She wasn't ready to go at all.

The house seemed uncomfortably quiet. Usually Sunday afternoons had a sweet peacefulness about them, especially when the kids were gone and he had the place all to himself. But instead of kicking back and watching a ball game, he was pacing like a caged beast, unable to sit still or focus.

Matt massaged his temple, trying to ease the tension building inside his skull. His children were with Shelby, learning she was leaving Dover and going back home. They were going to be heartbroken. Shelby believed his children would understand and accept her departure. He wasn't so sure. His kids adored Shelby. Every word out of their mouths was prefaced with her name. She would leave a big hole in their lives when she left. One he had no idea how to fill.

Walking out onto the porch, his gaze went immediately to the house next door. A few weeks ago his life had been calm, orderly and safe. Now his children's hearts were in danger and his own was shredded. He'd known from the start Shelby would go back to her career. So why did it hurt so much now that she was? Because he loved her, that's why. No matter how hard he tried to deny it, Shelby held his heart.

A heart that could fail and take her away without warning. The very idea plunged a razor-sharp knife into his gut. He might love Shelby, but he couldn't afford to love her. The risk was too great. It was best she was leaving. Once Shelby was gone, they could go back to their normal life and everyone would be better off in the long run.

He turned on his heel and went back inside and headed upstairs. As he passed Cassidy's room, he glanced in and frowned. The room was a mess. Clothes and shoes were strewn all over the floor. Nail polish bottles lay on top of scraps of homework papers. Schoolbooks, pencils and backpack were tossed carelessly on her desk. Her bed was unmade. A small table in the corner was bulging with junk, haphazardly covered with a sheet.

Matt grimaced. It was time for his little princess to clean her room. He pulled off the sheet and small pieces of paper fluttered onto the floor. A large book shifted to the edge of the card table. A photograph caught his eye. Katie. He looked closer. It was a picture of his wife and children taken at an Easter-egg hunt several years ago. What was it doing here? Matt sorted through the items on the table. Large pages held photos of Katie that the kids had decorated with tiny trinkets and ribbons. A scrapbook.

He'd seen Shelby working on her grandmother's

scrapbook during the weeks she'd been here. She'd told him it was her therapy since being displaced from her job. He could easily imagine Cassidy wanting to do one, too. She wanted to do everything Shelby did. She was wonderful with his kids. For all his concerns about her, she'd never once disappointed him.

He sat down on the edge of Cassidy's bed and looked through the book. He could detect Kenny's hand in several of the pages. Shelby's creativity was clearly visible, as well. He'd always envied her that ability. She found beauty in even ordinary things. It was as if she saw the world with different eyes than most people.

The doorbell echoed through the house. Quickly he replaced the items on the table and drew the sheet over them. Hurrying downstairs, he found his father waiting at the back door. "Hey, Dad. Is something wrong? News about Ty?"

Tom Durrant smiled. "Nope. I just left my best pair of sunglasses in your car." Matt retrieved the glasses and invited his dad inside. He didn't have to tell his father something was on his mind.

"So what's troubling you? Care to talk about it?"

Maybe a different point of view would help him sort things out. "Shelby's decided to go back to New York. She's leaving in a few days."

"Well, that's not much of a surprise, is it?" Tom took a can of soda from the fridge and opened it.

"No. It's probably for the best anyway. She took the kids for pizza to tell them. They'll be heartbroken. They really like her."

"Yes, they do. What about you? Will your heart be broken, too?"

"No." The look on his dad's face said he didn't believe him for a second. "Maybe. Some. But it can't work."

"Why? Because she has a medical condition?"

"It complicates things, yes."

"How so?"

"Because she is sick. She's had a heart attack. How can I ask my kids to accept a mother who could die? I can't put them through that again."

"So you do love her, then. I mean, if you're thinking about her being a mother to your kids."

Matt stood and walked to the sink. "No. I'm not. I mean, if it were just me, then maybe, but it's not."

"Let me get this straight. You love Shelby, but she has a minor medical condition and might die at some point, so you can't marry her because she's not perfectly healthy."

It sounded so callous and selfish when his dad said it.

"Tell me, do you regret marrying Katie? Do you regret having those two precious kids with her?"

"Of course not. I loved every minute of our life together."

"So if she'd never been a part of your life, what would you have missed?"

"Everything wonderful and—"

Tom rose and came to his side, resting a comforting hand on his shoulder. "Let go of the fear, son. It's time to move forward. Even Job received a new family out of God's grace. Give the Lord your broken heart. Let Him put the pieces back together."

How was it possible to love someone so much yet be so afraid of that love? And how did he let go of the fear of being hurt again? His dad was right about one thing. The Lord couldn't fix a broken heart if you didn't give Him all the pieces.

* * *

Shelby watched the stunned expressions on Cassidy and Kenny's faces, bracing for their response. She'd broken the news that she would be leaving Dover at the end of the week. Their sad little faces mirrored her own.

Cassidy tugged her straw up and down through the plastic lid. "Are you going back to New York?"

"Yes." Cassidy looked at her with wide blue eyes, eyes like her father's.

"Daddy kept telling us you'd leave one day. But I don't want you to."

A lump of sadness settled in her chest. She should have expected him to do that.

"Can't you stay here?" Kenny's voice was filled with pleading.

Shelby hugged him to her side. "I don't have a job here, sweetheart."

"You could do scrapbooks for people." Cassidy's sweet face lit up with hope.

"That's a good idea." Shelby chuckled. "Gramma has complained she has to go all the way to Jackson to find a good assortment of material." A local scrapbooking store might do well here. Dover was certainly big enough now to support such an endeavor. There were several available storefronts around the square, and she'd always wanted to start a business of her own. Except she couldn't stay here now. She turned her focus back to the children and their crestfallen expressions. "I know I didn't give you very good news, but I wanted tell you myself because that's what friends do."

Kenny's bottom lip stuck out. "Who's going to watch us after school?"

Cassidy nodded. "And what about our scrapbook? I can't do it without you, Miss Shelby."

"I'm sure my gramma will be happy to babysit. She was supposed to from the beginning, remember? I was only her helper. And I'll bet she'd love to help you finish the scrapbook, Cass."

"Don't you love us anymore?"

"Of course I do." She reached across the table and took Cassidy's hand. "I want you to know that no matter where I am, I will always love you and we'll always be friends. You can call me whenever you want to talk, and maybe you can come and visit me in New York. There's all kinds of cool things to do and see."

"Daddy won't bring us." Cassidy shook her head slowly.

She was probably right about that. "Then maybe your aunt Laura will bring you. She's my friend, too. Or I can come and visit you. Remember, my gramma still lives next door, and I don't think she's planning on moving away."

Kenny looked over at her with wide eyes. "Are you going to die?"

"What?"

Cassidy and Kenny exchanged glances. "We heard Gramma talking about you on the way home from the airport. She said you were sick. That you had a heart attack."

Shelby sighed. She should have anticipated this, but she wanted to spare them any unnecessary worry. "Yes. I did, but it wasn't a bad one. Just a very little one. Kind of a warning attack." She squeezed Kenny's little hand.

"So, it's not a sure thing. I mean, it's not like when Mom had cancer?" Cassidy asked, her eyes moist.

"No, it's not like that," Shelby reassured her quickly. "There's a lot I can do to stay healthy. I'll take medicine, I'll exercise and eat right and I'll be fine. There's a lot of heart disease in my family, so I have to be extra careful. Plus, I had a checkup and the doctor told me I'm much better." The doctor had adjusted her meds. And, while he was pleased with her improvement, he'd admonished her to continue watching her diet and exercise regularly. He'd also strongly recommended she avoid stress. He probably wouldn't approve of her decision to return to the hectic pace of her life in New York. But she had no other option.

"Well, we'd better get back home. It's a school night, remember."

"Will you still watch us tomorrow after school?"

She swallowed the lump of sadness in her throat. How could she face that final moment of goodbye? "Sure. I wouldn't miss that." Shelby gathered up the children and started toward the door, painfully aware of the dejected slope of their small shoulders. Seeing the fear in their eyes when they had asked about her health made her fully realize the depth of their grief in losing their mother. Maybe Matt was right. Having her in their lives wasn't a good thing. But how was she going to face leaving them?

The sun had barely topped the trees when Shelby gave up hope of sleeping. She'd spent the night wrestling between her heart and her common sense. Her heart longed to stay in Dover, be near Matt and the children, but her common sense told her that would cause pain for everyone. Today's meeting at Harmon Publishing had only added to her worries. Not since breaking up with Matt had she wanted so desperately to run and never look back. But she'd learned the hard way that running and avoiding only made things worse.

Tossing aside the covers, she rose and went to the window, pulling back the lace curtain to look at Matt's house. One afternoon was all she had left with Cassidy and Kenny. Gramma would be home tomorrow and she would take over the babysitting duties. A sob formed in the center of her chest. How she dreaded this day and that moment when she'd have to say goodbye. She'd decided to take the children to a movie that afternoon or to the park. Anything to keep her busy and out of Matt's house. Sitting there waiting for the end to come would be torture.

Sadness rose up without warning, swamping her like a tidal wave. The smallest thought of Cassidy and Kenny brought her to tears. Her heart burned like it was being slowly pulled from her chest. She couldn't allow herself to even think about Matt.

Turning away from the window, she prayed for courage and strength to face the challenges of the day. She had to stay busy today. Keep her mind occupied. After a quick shower and breakfast, she devoted herself to finishing the scrapbook as a welcome home for Gramma. She ached for her comforting hug. Being alone made all of this worse.

When her cell rang later in the morning she jumped. She'd been so absorbed in her task she'd forgotten about the meeting. One glance at the screen told her it was the call she'd been dreading. She answered, listening as her boss relayed the bad news, her heart sinking into the pit of her stomach.

Stunned, Shelby dropped her phone on the table and buried her face in her hands. Her worst fears had come true. No one at Harmon had been spared. *Tween Scene,* along with most other publications, was being discontinued. The new company was restructuring everything, moving in a different direction. Severance packages were generous but wouldn't last long. She'd have to find a different place to live, a new job. Her head throbbed with the enormity of the prospect.

She thought she'd been prepared for this moment, but now that it was here, it was more frightening than she'd expected. Her heart raced. Pressure began to build in her chest. A sob rose up from deep inside, doubling her over with its force. It was too much. Matt. The children. Her job. How was she supposed to go on when her life was in ruins?

Her throat tightened, making it hard to swallow. Closing her eyes, she shook her head, fighting the sense of impending doom crawling across her mind. She straightened and started across the room for a glass of water to calm her nerves. A wave of dizziness brought her up short. She couldn't catch her breath. A vice grip squeezed around her chest. Fear closed her throat. Her palms grew damp, broke out in a cold sweat.

Black fear rose up from her core, coiling along her nerves like a deadly serpent. "No. Oh, please, God. Not again." She couldn't be having a heart attack. She forced herself to remain calm and think. She'd been following orders, eating right, exercising, taking her meds. Why was this happening again?

What should she do now? Call the paramedics? The cardiologist she'd seen was an hour away in Jackson. Shelby closed her eyes, struggling to calm herself. Dr. Morgan had given her reams of information to read to educate herself on her medical condition. Why hadn't she read it?

One thought screamed loud and clear in her mind.

She didn't want to die. This wasn't about Matt or a job. This was about life and death.

Hurrying to the phone, she dialed 911, praying she hadn't waited too late.

Matt strode down the hall toward his office, eager to lock himself inside and grab a bite to eat. He was having a hard time concentrating on lessons today. He kept thinking about Shelby and her decision to leave Dover. It was for the best, but the thought of her being gone left a hollow feeling in his chest.

His cell phone rang the moment he grasped his office doorknob. The name displayed on the screen brought him up short. Pam Fleming. Why would she be calling him at work? A finger of concern touched his mind. "Hello."

"Matt, this is Pam Fleming, Shelby's friend."

"Yes, I know. What can I do for you?" There was a pause that sent Matt's concern spiking.

"I just found out that Shelby was brought in by ambulance earlier. They think she's had a heart attack."

Icy fear froze the blood in his veins. "Is she—"

"I don't know any more right now. I'm headed down to the E.R. to check on her. I thought you should know."

"Yes. Thanks. I'll come right over." His mind struggled to grasp what had happened. He had to get to the hospital. He had to see her, to know she was all right. Within minutes he was in his car heading for the hospital on the other side of town. He'd arranged for a replacement for his classes and called his mom to come stay with the kids after school.

Pulsing urgency coursed through him as he navigated traffic. Why was everyone driving so slowly today? He turned onto a side street, hoping to make better time on the lesser-traveled streets.

He'd feared this moment since Shelby had first told him of her heart problems and he'd tried to steel himself against this very thing. Yet here he was, living his worst nightmare. His heart pounded violently in his chest. If she died... He couldn't go through this again.

Flashing blue lights appeared up ahead and Matt slowed his speed, passing the group of vehicles on the side of the road. An ambulance was parked in front of a wrecked sedan. He sent up a prayer for the victims and another one for Shelby. It hit him then that it could have been her in that car. In fact, it could have been him. No one knew the number of days the Lord had assigned to them.

How many days had the Lord given to Shelby? What if this were the day He called her home? The thought rocked him to his core.

He loved Shelby. He'd admitted that, but not enough to risk committing his life to her. But if he lost her, his life from here on would be empty. He didn't want to live in fear any longer. He wanted to be happy again, and having her in his life would be worth the risk.

He knew the exact moment when he'd lost his heart to her again. Friday night in the middle of the pizza place. He'd turned to see Shelby at the table with his kids, relaxed, comfortable, as if she belonged there. He'd tried to deny it, but he'd known in that instant she belonged in his family, in his home and in his life.

He'd loved Katie; they'd been happy together. But she was gone. What kind of happiness would he miss out on if he kept Shelby out of his life? He didn't want to find out. He prayed for her life and for time to set things right between them.

The Lord had given them each a number of days. Wanted them to live in the present, allowing their faith to light the next step, not the next mile. He'd been relying on his own to protect his heart and those of his children. Dad was right. He couldn't prevent people from loving and caring about each other. It was time to trust in the Lord and make the most of this day.

Matt battled a gnawing fear as he followed the nurse through the emergency room corridors. No one would tell him anything, instructing him to talk to her physician. He tried to prepare himself for the worst, praying every second for the chance to tell her how he felt. The nurse stopped and pointed to a curtained-off cubicle. He stopped outside room 219, suddenly afraid of what he would find on the other side.

"Miss Russell, there's someone here to see you." She pulled back the curtain and walked away. Shelby was standing beside the bed, dressed and sorting through her purse. She turned, her beautiful brown eyes wide with surprise when she saw him.

"Matt?"

"I came as soon as I heard." He'd expected to find her in bed, pale and weak. Instead she looked as healthy as a fall rose. "What are you doing out of bed?"

"How did you know?"

"Pam called. Are you all right? They said you'd been brought in by ambulance. That you'd had a heart attack."

She smiled, further confusing him. "No. Well, they thought so at first, the tests confirmed that it was only an anxiety attack. Nothing to do with my heart at all. Just stress."

"Stress?"

She nodded, focusing on her purse again. "Yes. It's official. I'm out of a job. Guess I wasn't as prepared for the news as I'd thought."

"I'm sorry to hear that. So you're all right?"

"Fine. Sorry, I didn't mean to upset you."

"Upset?" He walked toward her, searching her eyes for confirmation that she was telling him the truth. He reached out and took her arms in his hands. "I was frantic. I thought you might be—" Relief surged through like a dam bursting. He pulled her into his arms, one hand cradling the back of her head. "I thought I'd lost you. Thank God you're all right." He held her face in his hands, his thumbs gently caressing her cheeks. For the first time in a long time, he felt whole. "Shelly—"

"Oops. So sorry, didn't mean to intrude."

Matt turned to see Pam Fleming in the doorway, a knowing smirk on her face.

"I was just coming to get our patient. Admissions has cleared you to leave, girlfriend."

"You're going home? Now?"

Shelby nodded. "No reason to keep me. Pam is going to drive me home."

Matt glanced over his shoulder. "No need. I can take her. She lives right next door, you know."

"Fine with me. I'll go get the wheelchair. And, yes, Shelby, you have to ride in it. It's hospital policy, so don't argue."

He looked at Shelby. Her eyes were filled with questions. He wanted to answer them all, but not here. Not now. He'd been a coward. So deeply wounded by Shelby's leaving and Katie's dying to risk his heart again. God had given them a second chance and he vowed to make the most of it.

The moment Matt parked his SUV beside the house, Shelby opened the door and climbed out. They hadn't spoken the entire way home. If she didn't get away from him soon she'd be in the throes of another anxiety attack. "Thank you for bringing me home." She tore her gaze from his handsome face and started toward Gramma's house.

"Shelby."

She turned reluctantly to face him. She raised her chin and met his gaze.

"Where are you going?"

There was a strange tone in his voice she'd never heard before. The truth pierced her heart. "I'm going home."

He moved closer, his blue eyes holding her gaze. "Why?"

"It's where I belong."

He stopped in front of her, so close she had to tilt back her head to see him. His nearness made her want to cry. Only a short time ago she was safe in his embrace. Now she had to walk away.

"I agree."

Her heart shriveled inside her chest. Nothing had changed. He still wanted her gone, out of his life. Tears filled her eyes and she turned away. Matt gently pulled her around to face him.

"What do you want from me, Matt?" She tried to pull away, but he held her tightly.

"That's not your home." He tightened his grip.

She tried to pull away again, but he held firm. "I'll be leaving in a few days. You were right, after all. It wasn't a heart attack, but it could have been."

"No. You're wrong."

Shelby shivered as he slid his hands slowly down her arms.

"Because if it hadn't happened, I would never have realized what a coward I was and I would have lost you a second time."

Shelby wasn't sure she'd heard him right. "I don't understand." She searched his eyes for some explanation.

"I love you, Shelly. I always have."

"No." She struggled to grasp what she was hearing. "You can't. What if—"

Matt pressed his fingers against her lips. "What if a plane falls on the house tomorrow? What if a storm blows everything away? We had no warning Katie was going to get sick. Ty didn't see those bullets coming. It happened. The same could happen to any of us any time. None of that matters. I love you. My children adore you. Whatever the future holds, we'll face it together. Your home is with us. Nowhere else."

Shelby wanted to believe what she saw in Matt's eyes, what he was saying, but she'd given up hope.

Matt brushed a strand of hair off her forehead. "All I could think of as I drove to town was how much we would have missed because of my stupid fear. How much joy my children would never know because I tried to protect them in the wrong way."

"Matt, are you sure?"

He grinned and pulled her into his embrace. "Yes. I know you love me, too. Don't you?"

She nodded against the warmth of his chest. "How did you guess?"

He chuckled softly. "Only a woman who loved me would help my children make a scrapbook about their mother."

"I do love you. I never stopped. I was such a fool to—"

Matt silenced her with a soft kiss. "That's in the past. I want to look to the future. Marry me?"

"I want to, but can you deal with my problem?"

Maybe he didn't understand what she'd told him. Maybe he wasn't thinking clearly.

"Can you deal with mine?" He leaned close and whispered in her ear, "I snore."

She stared at him a moment, then giggled. "That could be a deal breaker."

"Come home, Shelly. You belong with me. With us."

She looked into his eyes and saw her future. "I know."

* * * * *

*If you enjoyed this story by Lorraine Beatty,
be sure to check out the other books
this month from Love Inspired!*

Dear Reader,

I hope you enjoyed meeting Shelby and Matt and their small Mississippi town of Dover. It's always fun when old loves reunite and the sparks fly. And that's just what happens with these two. But old resentments and misconceptions can distort even the best relationships if we're not careful.

Trust and communication were key factors in Matt and Shelby's breakup and their reunion. Trusting God with our lives and communicating daily with Him through His word are vital to our faith journey.

I enjoyed writing Matt and Shelby's story because like many of us, they believed they were in control of their lives. We all have plans for our lives, visions of how things will unfold. But oftentimes we forget to ask God what His plans are for our lives, and I've learned we can never think up, create or envision a plan that is better than the one Our Father has laid out for us.

I enjoy hearing from readers. You can write me at LorraineBeatty.blogspot.com or through Love Inspired Books.

Lorraine Beatty

Questions for Discussion

1. Shelby is confronted with a health issue that forces her to return to her small hometown and make drastic changes in her lifestyle. Has a sudden illness or other life-changing event ever forced you in a new direction?

2. Matt was deeply wounded by his wife's death and Shelby's rejection many years ago. When Matt first sees Shelby again, his old wounds and resentments are reawakened. What does the Lord want us to do with old hurts?

3. Shelby broke her engagement with Matt fearing she would lose her dream. She put all her energy into her career. What happens when we put too much emphasis on the wrong things?

4. Matt is worried that Shelby will befriend his children then disappear, leaving them heartbroken the way she did him. Was Matt's fear warranted, or was he rationalizing his own fears of being hurt a second time?

5. Shelby set a course for her life without seeking the Lord's counsel. She believed her way was the best and expected God to bless her actions. Have you made plans for your life? What if God has a different plan?

6. As Shelby cares for Matt's children, she finds great joy and satisfaction, more than she ever experi-

enced in her dream career. Coming home to Dover has opened up new interests and options for Shelby. When God closes a door in your life, do you look around for a newly opened window?

7. Shelby worked in an environment where certain behaviors were accepted, even encouraged and admired. When she meets Matt's daughter, Cassidy, she begins to question whether chasing the world's ideas of beauty is appropriate. The world is always pushing the envelope of what is acceptable. Talk about a time when you were tempted to follow the world's ideas even when it went against what God's word instructed.

8. Matt realizes he's falling in love with Shelby again, but her heart disease is a huge barrier for him. He's lost a wife to cancer and to risk loving another woman who could die terrifies him. His fear and lack of faith are hampering his ability to love again. Fear can cripple our lives and block the blessings God has planned for us. What fears do you have that might be keeping you from happiness?

9. Matt's worst fears are realized when he learns Shelby has suffered another heart attack. He is forced to confront his fears at last and make a choice. Life without Shelby or life with her and all the risks that come with it. Have you faced a moment when you had to choose to let go of the fear and risk your heart?

10. Matt has fallen in love with Shelby once more and has begun to trust her again. But when she's late

showing up for his daughter's party, he immediately assumes the worst. How can jumping to conclusions and holding on to old resentments keep us from close relationships with others and with God?

11. Both Shelby and Matt thought they could control their lives by sheer will. Both ultimately failed. Talk about why it's so hard to give control of our lives over to the Lord and why we think we can manage our lives better than He can.

COMING NEXT MONTH from Love Inspired®
AVAILABLE APRIL 23, 2013

HER UNFORGETTABLE COWBOY
Cowboys of Sunrise Ranch
Debra Clopton
When competitive kayaker Jolie Sheridan returns to Sunrise Ranch, can she convince former fiancé Morgan McDermott that she's ready to take a second chance on a cowboy?

JOHANNA'S BRIDEGROOM
Hannah's Daughters
Emma Miller
Everyone in their Amish community knows widow Johanna Yoder and widower Roland Byler are meant to marry—but what will it take for the two of them to realize it?

THE LAWMAN'S SECOND CHANCE
Kirkwood Lake
Ruth Logan Herne
Widowed state trooper Alex Steele needs all the help he can get with his three kids, and lovely Lisa Fitzgerald is great with them. Dare he risk his heart again?

HEALING THE FOREST RANGER
Leigh Bale
If dealing with her troubled daughter wasn't bad enough, forest ranger Lyn Warner finds herself at odds with wild-horse representative Cade Baldwin—but soon the only thing she's fighting is her attraction.

HOMETOWN FIREMAN
Moonlight Cove
Lissa Manley
When dog rescuer Ally York meets handsome firefighter Drew Sellers, the walls she's built around her heart start to crumble. Only problem is, *neither* of their plans include love.

ALASKAN HERO
Teri Wilson
Rescue patrolman Brock Parker specializes in finding people buried under snow, but training Anya Petrova's timid dog makes him realize love may be what he's *really* searching for.

Look for these and other Love Inspired books wherever books are sold, including most bookstores, supermarkets, discount stores and drugstores.

LICNM0413

REQUEST YOUR FREE BOOKS!

2 FREE INSPIRATIONAL NOVELS
PLUS 2
FREE
MYSTERY GIFTS

Love Inspired

YES! Please send me 2 FREE Love Inspired® novels and my 2 FREE mystery gifts (gifts are worth about $10). After receiving them, if I don't wish to receive any more books, I can return the shipping statement marked "cancel." If I don't cancel, I will receive 6 brand-new novels every month and be billed just $4.49 per book in the U.S. or $4.99 per book in Canada. That's a saving of at least 22% off the cover price. It's quite a bargain! Shipping and handling is just 50¢ per book in the U.S. and 75¢ per book in Canada.* I understand that accepting the 2 free books and gifts places me under no obligation to buy anything. I can always return a shipment and cancel at any time. Even if I never buy another book, the two free books and gifts are mine to keep forever.

105/305 IDN FVV7

Name _____ (PLEASE PRINT) _____

Address _____ Apt. # _____

City _____ State/Prov. _____ Zip/Postal Code _____

Signature (if under 18, a parent or guardian must sign)

Mail to the **Harlequin® Reader Service:**
IN U.S.A.: P.O. Box 1867, Buffalo, NY 14240-1867
IN CANADA: P.O. Box 609, Fort Erie, Ontario L2A 5X3

**Are you a subscriber to Love Inspired books
and want to receive the larger-print edition?
Call 1-800-873-8635 or visit www.ReaderService.com.**

* Terms and prices subject to change without notice. Prices do not include applicable taxes. Sales tax applicable in N.Y. Canadian residents will be charged applicable taxes. Offer not valid in Quebec. This offer is limited to one order per household. Not valid for current subscribers to Love Inspired books. All orders subject to credit approval. Credit or debit balances in a customer's account(s) may be offset by any other outstanding balance owed by or to the customer. Please allow 4 to 6 weeks for delivery. Offer available while quantities last.

Your Privacy—The Harlequin® Reader Service is committed to protecting your privacy. Our Privacy Policy is available online at www.ReaderService.com or upon request from the Harlequin Reader Service.

We make a portion of our mailing list available to reputable third parties that offer products we believe may interest you. If you prefer that we not exchange your name with third parties, or if you wish to clarify or modify your communication preferences, please visit us at www.ReaderService.com/consumerchoice or write to us at Harlequin Reader Service Preference Service, P.O. Box 9062, Buffalo, NY 14269. Include your complete name and address.

LI13

SPECIAL EXCERPT FROM

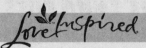

*Jolie Sheridan gets more than she bargained for
when she arrives at Sunrise Ranch for a teaching job.*

Read on for a preview of
HER UNFORGETTABLE COWBOY.

Jolie followed Morgan outside. There was a large gnarled oak tree still bent over as it had been all those years ago. She didn't stop until she reached it, turning his way only after they were beneath the wide expanse of limbs.

Morgan crossed his arms and studied the tree. "I remember having to climb up this tree and talk you down after you scrambled up to the top and froze."

She hadn't expected him to bring up old memories—it caught her a little off guard. "I remember how mad you were at having to rescue the silly little new girl."

A hint of a smile teased his lips, fraying Jolie's nerves at the edges. It had been a long time since she'd seen that smile.

"I got used to it, though," he said, his voice warming.

Electricity hummed between them as they stared at each other. Jolie sucked in a wobbly breath. Then the hardness in Morgan's tone matched the accusation in his eyes.

"What are you doing here, Jolie? Why aren't you taming rapids in some far off place?"

"I…I'm—" She stumbled over her words. "I'm taking a leave from competition for a little while. I had a bad run in Virginia." She couldn't bring herself to say that she'd almost died. "Your dad offered me this teaching opportunity."

"I heard about the accident and I'm real sorry about that, Jolie," Morgan said. "But why come here after all this time?"

"This is my *home*."

Jolie saw anger in Morgan's eyes. Well, he had a right to it, and more than a right to point it straight at her.

But she'd thought she'd prepared for it.

She was wrong.

"Morgan," Jolie said, almost as a whisper. "I'd hoped we could forget the past and move forward."

Heart pounding, she reached across the space between them and placed her hand on his arm. It was just a touch, but the feeling of connecting with Morgan McDermott again after so much time rocked her straight to her core, and suddenly she wasn't so sure coming home had been the right thing to do after all.

Will Morgan ever allow Jolie back into
his life—and his heart?

Pick up HER UNFORGETTABLE COWBOY
available May 2013 from Love Inspired Books.

Copyright © 2013 by Debra Clopton

LIEXP0413

Love Inspired

Will You Marry Me?

Bold widow Johanna Yoder stuns Roland Byler when she asks
him to be her husband. To Johanna, it seems very sensible that
they marry. She has two children, he has a son. Why shouldn't
their families become one? But the widower has never forgotten
his long-ago love for her; it was his foolish mistake that split
them apart. This could be a fresh start for both of them—until
she reveals she wants a marriage of convenience only. It's up to
Roland to woo the stubborn Johanna and convince her to accept
him as her groom in her home and in her heart.

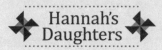

Hannah's
Daughters

Johanna's Bridegroom
by
Emma Miller

Available May 2013